INKED PERSUASION

A MONTGOMERY INK: FORT COLLINS NOVEL

CARRIE ANN RYAN

INKED PERSUASION

A Montgomery Ink: Fort Collins Novel

By
Carrie Ann Ryan

Inked Persuasion
A Montgomery Ink: Fort Collins Novel
By: Carrie Ann Ryan
© 2020 Carrie Ann Ryan
ISBN: 978-1-63695-095-2

Cover Art by Sweet N Spicy Designs
Photograph by Sara Eirew

PRAISE FOR CARRIE ANN RYAN

"Count on Carrie Ann Ryan for emotional, sexy, character driven stories that capture your heart!" – Carly Phillips, NY Times bestselling author

"Carrie Ann Ryan's romances are my newest addiction! The emotion in her books captures me from the very beginning. The hope and healing hold me close until the end. These love stories will simply sweep you away." ~ NYT Bestselling Author Deveny Perry

"Carrie Ann Ryan writes the perfect balance of sweet and heat ensuring every story feeds the soul." - Audrey Carlan, #1 New York Times Bestselling Author

"Carrie Ann Ryan never fails to draw readers in with passion, raw sensuality, and characters that pop off the page. Any book by Carrie Ann is an absolute treat." – New York Times Bestselling Author J. Kenner

"Carrie Ann Ryan knows how to pull your heartstrings and make your pulse pound! Her wonderful Redwood Pack series will draw you in and keep you reading long into the night. I can't wait to see what comes next with the new generation, the Talons. Keep them coming, Carrie Ann!" – Lara Adrian, New York Times bestselling author of CRAVE THE NIGHT

"With snarky humor, sizzling love scenes, and brilliant, imaginative worldbuilding, The Dante's Circle series reads as if Carrie Ann Ryan peeked at my personal wish list!" – NYT Bestselling Author, Larissa Ione

"Carrie Ann Ryan writes sexy shifters in a world full of

passionate happily-ever-afters." – *New York Times* Bestselling Author Vivian Arend

"Carrie Ann's books are sexy with characters you can't help but love from page one. They are heat and heart blended to perfection." *New York Times* Bestselling Author Jayne Rylon

Carrie Ann Ryan's books are wickedly funny and deliciously hot, with plenty of twists to keep you guessing. They'll keep you up all night!" USA Today Bestselling Author Cari Quinn

"Once again, Carrie Ann Ryan knocks the Dante's Circle series out of the park. The queen of hot, sexy, enthralling paranormal romance, Carrie Ann is an author not to miss!" *New York Times* bestselling Author Marie Harte

CHAPTER 1

Annabelle

I was going to shake my hips, dance, and drink the night away. Okay, perhaps not the last thing, but I would drink a little.

I grinned over at my sister, Paige, who smiled widely back. I gave her a little wave. She leaned into her new boyfriend, Colton, joy evident in her expression. I didn't know this Colton, but he was brave for coming to a Montgomery event so fresh into their relationship. Even at a bar on a weekend night—seemingly an innocent time. But when it came to the Montgomerys and how we circled our prey, no time was innocent.

"You are staring at Paige like you are ready to grill her new boyfriend."

I looked up at my big brother, Beckett, and smiled.

"Maybe I am. After all, this is the first time she's brought him to a family event. It's a big thing."

Beckett shook his head and pushed his dark hair away from his face. He needed a haircut, so did his twin, Benjamin, but the two of them seemed to be going for a mountain man look. Soon, their beards would be annoyingly bushy, rather than what was on-trend these days. Of course, we were in Fort Collins, Colorado, not in Boulder or down in Denver with some of the other Montgomery cousins. We had standards when it came to facial hair. Not that I actually believed that, but I knew some of our friends did.

"Now you're grinning. Are you thinking of something evil?" Beckett asked.

I leaned my head on his shoulder and sighed. "Just thinking about the cousins."

"Which ones?" He sounded a little nervous, and I frowned, looking up at him. "We like all of our cousins. I can't even say *most* because we *actually* do like them all. What's with the tone?"

He shook his head, wrapped his arm around my shoulders, and pulled me closer to him. He smelled like sandalwood and soap. He must have showered before he came out to join us at Riggs'. He had been out on the grounds all day, all of us working hard to finish up the last bit of the leading project before we started on the new, larger one that had also been keeping me up at night.

"Dad was grumbling about something the other Montgomerys did, and I'm not in the mood to talk about it. We are here to drink, have fun, and grill not only this new Colton but our baby brother's new beau, as well."

"Did you say 'beau?'" Benjamin asked, frowning as he walked toward us. Beckett flipped him off.

Benjamin was the mirror image of Beckett. Why my parents decided to give both sets of twins similar names, I would never know.

Beckett and Benjamin had been born first, and then Archer and I came next. If anything, they should have given the older brothers names starting with A, and then Archer and I should have gotten B names. But wanting to go alphabetical had not been in the cards, apparently.

Our baby sister Paige was the only one of us without a twin. And, sadly, she did not have a name that started with a C, much to her consternation. She'd even tried to go as a Chloe or Christine for a while when we were younger, but she always ended up as Paige.

When Beckett and I didn't answer him in time, Benjamin cleared his throat. "What are you guys talking about?"

Beckett shrugged. "Nothing, just Dad being a jerk. And now I am getting ready to be by Annabelle's side when we grill the two new people who've joined us tonight."

Benjamin shook his head and raised his brow at his older brother. "You know, you said the word *beau*, and that's not a word I think has ever left your mouth before."

Beckett's lips twitched, and I grinned. The two of them usually took turns being the broodiest. Generally, they had scowls under those beards and rarely smiled or laughed. I wasn't sure why they were always so serious. Maybe they'd been a little less severe as babies. And then Archer and I had shown up and probably terrorized the twins. I might not be as wild as Archer, or as carefree—I couldn't be, not after everything that had happened—but I still smiled a lot more than Benjamin and Beckett did.

Paige was a unique delight. Which was exactly how she liked and wanted it, even if she *had* said at one point that she

3

wished she had a twin. She was the brightest one of us all, the happiest, and the sweetest. At least that's what I thought. Paige called me sweet, though usually when she was making fun of me for being weird. Because I *was* weird. I couldn't help it. I was a Montgomery.

"Okay, there's Archer and his boyfriend, Marc. Now we have the two youngest and their new *beaus*," Benjamin said, and Beckett flipped him off again.

"We're not actually going to terrorize them, are we?" I asked. "Because I kind of want our siblings to be happy."

Beckett raised a brow and shook his head. "Oh, they can be happy—once they pass our test."

"We're still learning how to do this whole big brother and sister thing when it comes to our siblings' relationships," Beckett explained and then held up three fingers, getting the bartender's attention. Riggs gave Benjamin a wink before pouring three shots of tequila.

I shook my head. "I swear, everywhere you go, everyone loves you."

Benjamin didn't smile, but he did snort. "No, that would be Archer. I just learned how to give that come-hither look to bartenders from our baby brother."

Beckett and I burst out laughing.

"And if you ever tell anyone I said that, I will hunt you down," Benjamin warned.

I shook my head, picked up my shot, and downed it. I closed my eyes and winced but didn't reach for salt or lime. Doing a tequila shot with the type of tequila Benjamin liked did not usually require salt or lime. And the twins would make fun of me if I asked for them. Of course, it was all out of love. But still, I wasn't about to open myself for teasing.

I looked across the crowd at the bar to our two siblings

and their significant others. "I think we should start with Paige and Colton. They seem to be more serious."

Beckett nodded. "I agree. They've also had at least three weeks longer than Archer and Marc."

Benjamin sighed. "I swear we should have started taking notes or something so we knew exactly how to interrogate them to make sure they're good enough for our baby siblings."

I smiled and listened as my brothers went through their plans. I might be Archer's twin, but I always felt a little more protective of him, a little older than the five minutes that separated us. Though he likely thought the same of me.

"You think that's too much?" Benjamin asked, frowning.

Beckett shook his head. "No, we need to get this right. After all, we've never had to deal with serious relationships before. While the rest of the Montgomerys got married, we've all stayed single. We need to get ready for the first marriage, you know?"

Both of the twins froze and risked glances at me.

I gave them a soft smile and shook my head. "Exactly," I said, not daring to broach that subject. "We need to get ready and interrogate these two new people who dared to step out with our siblings."

"Okay, now I'm a little afraid of what you guys are talking about," my twin said as he came towards us. He leaned down and kissed my cheek, his hand holding Marc's.

Archer looked like a slightly smaller version of Beckett and Benjamin. He wasn't as wide, and he didn't have a beard at the moment. But he had the same startling blue eyes and wicked grin. Not that the older twins showed those grins often, but when they did, they looked just like Archer.

I looked like him, too—after all, we were twins. But I was

a little softer around the edges, though my jaw was slightly more pointed than Paige's. We all looked like Montgomerys —both sides of the family.

My mother's maiden name was also Montgomery. She was the youngest sister of the Colorado Montgomerys, a completely different line than my father's. It made things a little weird for my dad. But having those connections meant we had dozens of cousins around the country, even more than *my* cousins, who lived close by.

"I feel like I should be scared," Marc said, grinning.

He was blond-haired, brown-eyed, and beautiful. *Shockingly* beautiful if I were honest. He was slender, wore well-cut pants, and a button-up shirt tucked in. At some point, he had rolled up his sleeves so his forearms showed, and I noticed he had a small tattoo peeking out. I wondered if one of our cousins had inked him, even though it was a vast country and world, and anybody could have done it. Still, I liked the idea that a Montgomery may have inked his skin.

"You should be scared," I said, leaning forward as Marc kissed my other cheek.

"I'll try to be. However, I think I overheard that you're going to take care of Paige's new guy first. This is great. I can watch how it happens and study the dynamics." Marc grinned, then wrapped his arm around Archer's waist. My twin beamed.

I loved that it looked as if Archer were falling in love. He appeared so happy. And if Marc hurt him, I would find a way to make the man scream in pain and agony while the other siblings took care of him.

Because nobody hurt my twin.

"You're looking a little vicious over there," Archer whispered, and I grimaced.

"Sorry, just thinking of weird things. And, Marc? You should still be wary. Because while we may practice certain techniques on Paige's new guy, you have your own set of rules."

Beckett nodded. "She's right. We have lists."

Benjamin nodded, his gaze on Marc, and Marc looked between all of us before he rocked back on his heels.

"You guys are a little scary when you're all together."

I looked at my brothers, and we all burst out laughing. "We're not that bad. I promise."

"They will not be that bad," Archer warned, and I didn't know if the warning was for Marc or us.

Finally, Paige tugged her boyfriend off the dance floor and skipped over to us, the smile on her face radiant. "Well, hello. Are you all talking about how you're going to maim and torture poor Colton and Marc for daring to come near your baby siblings?" she asked in a singsong. She leaned into Colton, and the big redheaded man rolled his eyes.

"You need to let them think they're all secretive with their glowering, darling," Colton said, kissing the top of her head.

"Oops," Paige said, giggling.

Everybody looked so damn happy, and I couldn't help but be content as well. I might not have the same type of connections they did with another human being right now, but I didn't need that. I'd nearly had a chance before, and I wasn't about to do that again. However, I could still have fun. And we were all happy, healthy, and here.

That was all that mattered.

"Okay, one more shot as a family, and then I'm dancing."

"That sounds like a plan," Archer said before meeting the bartender's gaze over my head.

I resisted the urge to roll my eyes as Archer gave that

same look Benjamin had stolen. Riggs poured a round of shots for everybody, and immediately after, the family was on the dance floor.

My brothers did their best to block me in, stopping anybody from daring to come near. I slowly moved away, rolling my eyes.

"You know, if you keep letting them pin you in, you'll never get to dance with a guy," Paige said, taking my hand. "What about the bartender? Riggs?" She gestured over to the man with his honey eyes and wicked grin.

"I'm pretty sure he only has eyes for Benjamin. And maybe Archer. Not so much for me."

"His eyes were on your butt. I'm pretty sure he swings for any Montgomery," Paige corrected.

"Well, my gaze doesn't swing that way—at least not tonight. I want to have fun and not deal with men or egos or penises or anything of the sort."

Colton's eyes widened as he came up from behind Paige and slowly raised his hands before backing away.

I winced. "You are going to have to explain to Colton that I didn't mean to just blurt out the word *penis* like that." I blinked. "Or now. Again."

Paige put her hand over her mouth, her eyes wide. "Annabelle," she mock-whispered.

"I'm sorry. Go. Fix it. I'm not crazy. I promise."

"You know, that's what they all say," Paige said solemnly before grinning again. She kissed my cheek and moved off to her boyfriend.

I danced with two of my brothers and then between another group of women who had come in for a good night. I felt free. I might not have a boyfriend or anybody on the horizon, but that was fine. Honestly, I didn't need that in my life. I had my family, a job I loved, and a massive project coming up that I needed to focus on.

I didn't need any more complications.

By the time the night wound down, my feet ached, and I regretted my shoes. But they made my butt look great, and I felt sexy in them. Sometimes, a girl just needed to feel good. I sat in the passenger seat as Benjamin drove me home. He'd only had one drink for the night, and I'd had three. It only made sense.

"Thanks for being the DD tonight," I said softly.

"Thank you for not taking off your shoes in my car because I know you want to," he said wryly. "You know I hate feet."

He didn't, but he liked making fun of me. I stuck out my tongue at him. "Weirdo," I teased.

"Maybe. But as I'm the one who is driving, and it's my car, you get to follow my rules. And I'll do you the courtesy of not taking off my shoes in your car when *my* feet hurt."

I grinned and shook my head. We pulled into my driveway, and Benjamin looked over at the house to my right. "Looks like your new neighbor moved in."

I nodded. "These houses get gobbled up fast, even in this housing market."

"It's a boom right now, hence why I have a job," my brother, the landscape architect, said. "But I'm sad your previous neighbor had to move away."

"Me, too. I liked her. Hopefully, this new person is just as quiet, doesn't have forty kids that will be in my yard, and is a happy person."

"You know we're going to end up becoming those crotchety old people who hold brooms and tell kids to get off their lawns."

"Well, if they would stop playing in my yard and play in theirs, it wouldn't be a problem," I said, laughing.

"You're talking to a man who works on landscapes for a living, I understand." He kissed the top of my head before I got out of the car.

"Thank you," I said.

"Be careful," Benjamin added, and I resisted the urge to roll my eyes.

My brothers acted like I could be snatched off the street in front of my home while they watched. But I was careful. I put my key in the lock, walked inside, and then turned and waved as Benjamin drove off. I let out a breath and then frowned as I looked over at the phonebook on my driveway. I hadn't noticed it being delivered earlier, and I didn't want it outside all night. I sighed and went to pick it up.

"Hey."

I whirled, dropped my keys, and tripped over my heels. I fell on my ass, the pavement digging into my palms. I looked up at the man silhouetted against the moonlight.

"Crap. I'm sorry. I didn't mean to startle you or freak you out. I was just letting you know that I was out here, headed into my house. But I accidentally scared you anyway." He held up a hand, and I looked at him, not wanting to go near him. "Seriously, let me help you up. I promise I'll stand here, and you can go back inside. Only wanted to say hello. I'm your new neighbor."

I frowned, feeling like I knew that voice, but I didn't know from where. Or how.

He could be a serial killer. If I kept sitting there, he could still try to kill me. I knew I should at least act like I knew what I was doing and not appear scared. I'd probably be able to fight him off better if I were standing. Maybe. I slid my hand into his and let him help me up. I dusted off my butt and then moved back a few steps, needing space.

My heart thudded, and my ankle hurt more as if I had twisted it.

"I am sorry," the man repeated. "Anyway, as I said, I'm your new neighbor. Jacob. Jacob Queen."

Ice slid over me as he stepped into the beam from my porch light. I did the same, my past coming at me full force. I swallowed hard, trying to catch my breath.

No, it couldn't be this. Not in the house I had built. Not in my family's neighborhood, the one we'd put our blood, sweat, and tears into.

This couldn't be Jacob. He couldn't be back.

But as he looked at me, his face suddenly devoid of color, I knew he recognized me. I knew this was the same Jacob.

"You," he whispered.

"You," I echoed.

And then he glowered at me, turned on his heel, and stomped away.

I couldn't help but look at the back of the man who had grown up with my late husband. His brother. And the one man in the whole world I knew hated me more with each and every breath.

CHAPTER 2

Jacob

I couldn't sleep. I stared up at the ceiling, the morning light shining around the closed blinds of my window. My eyes ached, and my heart hurt. Everything was just a little too much at the moment.

And, truthfully, I only had myself to blame.

How could I not have known she would be here?

Fort Collins wasn't a tiny one-horse town despite the jokes by others in the state and anyone who hadn't heard of the city. I shouldn't have ended up next door to the one person I never wanted to see. The one person who grated on me, got under my skin, and made me feel as if I had lost everything all over again. The one person who reminded me that I hadn't had enough time, and that fate was cruel.

And now, I couldn't get rid of her. I'd signed on the dotted line of my mortgage, and I owned every inch of the place I lived in. I couldn't give it back, say the place was faulty and run away.

I should've known there'd be a damn Montgomery next door. They were everywhere. They had even done some of my ink. I'd been down in New Orleans, visiting friends and trying to forget who I was, and decided I wanted a new tattoo. I had gone into a shop, found the best artist there, and discovered it was one of Annabelle Montgomery's cousins. I shouldn't have been surprised that it was a Montgomery, even in a different damn state.

I wore their ink on my flesh, and their scars on my soul.

I ran a hand over my beard, annoyed with myself, and was grateful when the alarm went off. I groaned, turned off the alert on my phone, and rolled out of bed. My toes pressed against the hardwood, and I stretched my neck, telling myself that an hour here or there was enough sleep to survive. I had a lot of shit to do, including unpacking. First, however, I needed to see my parents and get to work.

I was moving my law practice up north. Maybe not the best business decision, considering I had done pretty damn well for myself down in Denver, but my family needed me. And it was about time I was there for them again after running away so long ago.

I cursed myself once more, unplugged my phone from its charger, and made my way to the bathroom. I brushed my teeth, did my business, and headed to the shower, pretending like I wasn't breaking inside.

I should have known the memories would come at me hard. Every time I closed my eyes these days, I pictured my baby brother, Jonah, grinning up at me. Even when he was in pain.

But the damned woman—*girl* at the time—was all tangled

up in those memories, and I hated her for it. She had no right to be there or in my thoughts. She had no right to be in my past to begin with.

And now she lived next door, and I couldn't get away from her. I knew she still saw my parents, had wheedled her way into their lives, as well. And given our current situation, I would have to deal with her on an almost daily basis unless I wanted to lose money and sell the house right away. The housing market was doing well enough that I could probably do it and make a couple of bucks. Only not enough to cancel out the pain of moving again, finding another home, and dealing with my parents when they asked why I was picking up and leaving after only staying in my current house for less than a fucking week.

I rinsed the conditioner out of my hair, ran the soap over my body, and growled at myself as I finished showering. I shut off the water, reached for my towel, and dried off before stepping onto my bathmat.

The fucking *gall* of her to look at me as if she had seen a ghost. How dare she look at me as if I would hurt her? She was the one who had ruined everything. Had taken precious time and energy from Jonah. My baby brother hadn't needed her complications. But she had seemed to want the fucking limelight and hadn't allowed me the time I needed with my brother before he was gone. I would never fucking forgive her for that.

I let out a breath, closed my eyes, and counted to ten. I had to stop being so angry. I had left Fort Collins to attend college elsewhere, so I *could* stop being angry. I took out loans, stayed in school, and went to a state college so my parents didn't have to spend what little money they had left after Jonah's diagnosis and life in and out of hospitals. I hadn't taken a dime from them, even though they'd offered. Because I hadn't wanted to take any more from them. They'd already lost enough.

But it seemed they always had Annabelle. *My brother's widow.*

What a fucking crock.

I got dressed and did my best not to stay angry. I'd been to plenty of therapy sessions and talked to enough bartenders to get myself through and get on with what I needed to do. I didn't need to be an angry, obsessed man. I just needed to get through my day, help my mother and father, and work my ass off. I didn't need to think about Annabelle Montgomery—or any other name she chose to use. I didn't even know if her name was ever Annabelle Queen.

"Hell," I mumbled to myself.

Had she taken my brother's name? Did she have *my* name? Chills slid up my back, and I shook them off. Whatever. I needed to stop thinking about that.

The doorbell rang, and I swallowed hard, hoping it was an overeager postal carrier. But as I opened the door, I knew I wasn't so lucky.

Annabelle smiled up at me and held out a pink box from a very familiar place. "The best donuts in the state. As a peace offering for looking like a scared deer in headlights last night when I saw you outside."

I looked down at the box, and then at her face, and did my best not to slam the door. "I don't need a peace offering or whatever the hell you think this is."

She paled a bit, her lips pressing into a thin line before she put on a whole new persona like a mask, as if she weren't an angry woman trying to win me over. Instead, she seemed happy and bubbly as if she hadn't a care in the world. Maybe she didn't. Perhaps she didn't miss my brother as I did.

It wouldn't surprise me. It wasn't like she knew him. No, she had only married him for the press.

"Well, I wanted to welcome you to the neighborhood. This is the Montgomery neighborhood, by the way," she said through gritted teeth, even though she was smiling.

Dread filled me. She couldn't be saying what I thought she was. "What?" I asked.

"My family? Montgomery Builders? We built every single one of these homes. We all live here, too, though on different blocks. So, even though our name isn't on the stonework out front for the community, it's still our place. And...welcome to it."

The Montgomerys had built this place? The one development that'd called to me when I did a quick search of the area while looking to find a neighborhood near my parents. Of course, they had. And they surrounded me.

Like they always did.

"I see."

"Well, I don't really think *I* see." She looked down at the box in her hands and let out a breath. "Jacob, it's been a long time. I just wanted to say good morning and welcome. We're going to be neighbors for a while now, unless you move away tomorrow."

"I thought about it," I growled.

Her eyes widened. "How can you hate me so much that you would think about leaving the home you just moved into?"

"I can hate you for a lot of reasons."

"No, you can't. Stop being an idiot. It's not my fault you

didn't realize that my family built this place. It's probably on all of the documents you signed."

"Didn't see your name."

"Then you weren't looking. You never did see the things that were right in front of you."

I narrowed my eyes at her. "You want to hash this out?"

"Maybe we should. Because I'm not a huge fan of under-currents, and you've always been a snide little brat to me."

I clenched my fist, and her gaze moved to it. I let my hand relax and met her gaze. "I hate you," I whispered.

She didn't stagger back, but she did swallow hard. "I don't know why. I miss him, too."

"Do you? I don't know if I believe that." She shook her head, her hands digging into the pink box. I sighed. "Here, give me that. I don't want you to ruin perfectly good donuts."

"I don't know if you deserve these now."

"You don't really have a choice, do you? They were a gift." I grabbed the box from her and then took a step inside to set them on the table. I didn't invite her in, and she didn't move forward as if she wanted to come inside. I didn't know if I blamed her. My alcove was deep and shady enough that unless someone were at Annabelle's house, they wouldn't be able to overhear what we were saying. But if a neighbor had binoculars or something, they could prob-ably see her standing there despite the shadows. I didn't care what my neighbors thought about me, though. Not now.

"Jonah and I married because he loved me, and I loved him. Maybe not in the way of most adults, but we knew that we didn't marry for the same kind of love your parents had— or even mine."

"You were only using him."

She blanched and shook her head. "Never. I promise you. Jonah was my best friend."

"Really? I know that's what you kept telling the press. They ate it up."

"Because it's the truth," she spat. "Jonah had cystic fibrosis. You know that. You *knew*, just like I did, that he wouldn't make it past his eighteenth birthday. The doctors didn't even think he would make it past his thirteenth."

"You don't have to remind me," I shouted, then let out a breath and took a step inside. "Come in. I'm not in the mood to make someone call the cops."

She glared at me and moved past the threshold, and I closed the door behind her. I didn't lock it. Even in my current state, I wanted to make sure she knew she was safe from me physically. I wasn't locking her in or anything. Yet I didn't even know if she registered that action.

"You don't have to tell me what happened with my brother. I know he was sick. I watched him slowly die for his entire life."

"But he *lived* it, too. Don't forget that. He smiled, laughed, learned. He brought so much to this world, and all he wanted was a wedding. You know he was a romantic. He dreamed of weddings and the perfect love and everything that he knew he'd never get to have. So I gave that to him." She raised her chin. "Other people might not have understood, but I always thought you would. He was your brother. Didn't you understand that he wanted what we had?"

"You weren't his real wife," I bit out.

"Of course, not," she whispered. "But I was his *wife*. Because he asked. And because my best friend was dying, and I loved him. I would have done anything to put a smile on his face in those last days. Anything," she said, her voice breaking. "You know how much pain he was in. He just needed something, and I gave him what I could."

I pinched the bridge of my nose, trying not to look at her tears. I hated them. I didn't think they were weapons right now, but I'd thought they were when we were younger. I'd thought she used them for the cameras. But as I looked at her here, I wondered if maybe everything I'd assumed before was wrong. Perhaps she wasn't a person who needed the limelight. But I didn't know.

I really hated those tears. They may look real now, but I didn't know what to think. Still, I hated her.

"I hated you for so long," I bit out. "Jonah was all about you. Everything that he did in the end was for you and about you. He pushed us away."

Annabelle reached out, then let her hand fall. "I didn't realize it at the time," she whispered. "I didn't realize that everything was so weird and different. I was only trying to help my best friend. I didn't know I was hurting you or anyone else in the process. Jacob, I'm sorry."

"I don't think sorry is going to cut it. It never did. You paraded yourself out there in front of the news media as the virgin bride, the perfect, young, eighteen-year-old still in high school, marrying her high school sweetheart."

"I hated the press. I hated everything. But your parents asked me to do it because it helped to raise money. You know that."

I held back a flinch. "What?" I asked.

She shook her head. "It's nothing."

"No. What are you talking about?"

"There was a fund to help with the last of the bills. With so many. And the more Jonah's story was out, the more people cared. And it helped him and the others in the center.

I did what I had to in order to follow his last wishes. But you were there, too. I'm sorry I took moments from you and him. I'm sorry I can't give them back. But *he's* not coming back. I can't bring him back. I would do anything to make Jonah come back. He was my best friend," she repeated. "I don't know what to do. I know you hate me, and I can't change that. But you're my neighbor now, and you'll just have to deal with the fact that I live here."

"You need to go," I whispered, trying to get my thoughts in order.

"Fine," she spat. "You know what? It's fine." She stormed past me, slamming the door behind her. I looked down at my hands, wondering what the hell I was going to do.

She had married my brother, given him five days of pure happiness as a husband and a man with a future. Five days of marriage, and then my brother died. And I hadn't been there because he'd said he needed time with his precious Annabelle.

I had lost time with my sibling. I'd lost so much. I hadn't been there.

Unfortunately, I couldn't even hate her as much as I felt I should.

I could only hate myself.

CHAPTER 3

Annabelle

"That stupid, self-serving son of a bitch," I snapped, pacing my office.

"Why don't you tell me how you really feel?" Paige said from beside me, and I rolled on her.

"Don't say that in your happy little voice. Be angry *with* me."

"I don't know who you want me to be angry at," Paige said, handing over my coffee.

"Why? Why are you handing me this?" I asked, taking it from her.

My sister shook her head. "Because you haven't even had a sip since you walked in here, and you need more caffeine."

"I'm shaking with rage, and you want to give me more energy?" I asked dryly.

She beamed at me. "Well, if you lose any of your caffeine

intake, you'll only get grouchier, and I'm not in a mood to handle that. So, take a sip, breathe, and tell me who I need to help you castrate."

I blinked at her, then took a sip of my coffee. "We just went straight to castration, then?" I asked.

"If that's what we need to do, then I will learn. Do we use scissors, a knife, or a sword? What do they use these days?" Paige asked, and I visibly shivered.

"We're not doing that, and you went really dark quickly."

"I'm going to blame Archer for that. We watched this medieval show with subtitles. I didn't understand it, but there was a whole scene about it, and now I'll never be able to sleep again." She shuddered, and I took another gulp of my coffee, wondering where I went wrong.

"You're scaring me. Archer always scares me, but now you're starting to scare me, too."

"I can't help it. It was a double date." She gave me a slow smile.

"I guess Marc and Colton are doing well?" I asked, wanting to know a little bit more about my siblings' boyfriends.

"Well, I can't speak for Archer and Marc, but Colton and I are doing well. Okay, enough about me," Paige said, rolling her shoulders back. "Who do we hate?"

"Jacob Queen moved into the house next door."

Paige blinked before plopping down in the chair in front of my desk. "Jacob? That Jacob?"

"Yes, that Jacob."

"Please tell me he's at least gotten ugly and gross and has lost all of that beautiful hair of his or something. Maybe developed smoking and now has yellow teeth?"

I shook my head. "I don't know why that matters, but

none of those. And because the gods hate me, he's broader than before, all muscle. And I think he's taller. Or maybe I've shrunk, I'm not sure. But his hair is just as thick as before, wavy at the ends. And he still has that damn jawline. It's the same Jacob Queen. The only man in the world who hates me."

"That was a lot of descriptions for a man you want me to help you castrate," Paige said nonchalantly.

I narrowed my eyes at her. "First off, we're not going to castrate Jacob Queen."

"That's not something I expected to hear today," Archer said as he walked in, eyebrows raised. "I mean, I don't know if I should help with that, considering it'd be a horrible thing, but I *could*. Paige and I recently watched a movie that included it."

"Please stop talking about castration," I snapped.

"Okay then, it seems I've come at a bad time," Benjamin said, Beckett behind him. I set my coffee down on my desk and put my hands over my face so I could silently scream into them.

"Annabelle is having a bad day, and we need her to finish that cup of coffee."

"How many cups has she had?" Beckett asked.

"This is her first."

"Dear God, get more caffeine into her," Archer said.

I narrowed my eyes at all of them as I lowered my hands. "I hate you. All of you."

"Not as much as you hate Jacob Queen," Beckett corrected.

"Please, stop it. All of you."

Another person walked into the room, and I narrowed my eyes at Beckett's new assistant project manager, Clay.

"I thought we had a meeting about the upcoming project, but if we're going to talk about castration, I think I'm going to head out," Clay said cautiously.

I shook my head, rolled my shoulders back, and did my best to become Annabelle Montgomery, Lead Architect of Montgomery Builders. Not broken, weary, and confused Annabelle of Jacob's past. "No, this is a work environment, and we are not going to discuss...that. Instead, we're going to go through the major projects we have coming up."

"First, I want to hear about the fact that Jacob Queen moved into the house next door," Paige said, and I could've thrown my coffee at her. It wasn't scorching, and it wouldn't hurt her. But it would startle her and make me feel better. Yes, startling would be nice.

"Jacob, who?" Clay asked.

"*That* Jacob?" Archer inquired. "Oh, God. I'm sorry."

"It's fine," I said.

"You know, I'm going to get some coffee. I'll be right back," Clay said, turning on his heel and practically running out of the office.

"Great, we scared the new guy." I sighed.

"He's tough. Storm introduced us. If he can handle the Denver Montgomerys, he can handle us," Beckett said.

I threw my hands up into the air. "Okay, we're going to put this out there into the world, and then we're not going to talk about it again."

"Why don't I believe that?" Beckett asked.

I pointed my finger at him and narrowed my eyes. "No. Stop it. No sarcasm."

"That's just not going to happen in this family," Archer said, sarcasm dripping from his tone.

"Anyway," I said, ignoring my twin, "Jacob Queen moved

into the house next door. And he still hates me. Told me to my face. And almost said no to donuts."

"From the pink box place?" Paige asked, her eyes wide.

I gave a tight nod. "From the pink box place."

"That's sacrilege," Archer whispered.

"I know. He took them, but I'm pretty sure he probably tossed them. He didn't want them, didn't want me in the house. Though after he started yelling, he didn't want to deal with cops more, so I followed him in. The donuts were still on the entry table when I left."

That made my brothers blow up, and all of them started shouting at once.

"I'm fine," I yelled over them.

"Excuse me?" Beckett cut in. "That asshole had the nerve to yell at you, and instead of dealing with cops, something we're going to talk about, you just walked into his house?"

I grimaced. "It's not how it sounded. I was perfectly safe. He didn't even lock me in." I blinked as Beckett's, Benjamin's, and Archer's eyes all narrowed.

Paige winced beside them and shook her head, mouthing, *please stop.*

Archer might be my twin, and I might be a couple of minutes older than him, but they all acted like my big, overbearing brothers sometimes. It was a little ridiculous. Paige and I had to deal with them and their macho tendencies in many instances. Usually, I could deal with it, but I was a little shaken after seeing Jacob that morning and discussing what had happened with Jonah. But now, I had a feeling I would have to discuss it again.

"You guys do not have to do anything. I promise. We talked it out...sort of. He'll likely continue to hate me, but we'll just deal with being neighbors. Not everybody has to like who lives next door."

"He has no right to hate you," Benjamin growled.

"No right," Beckett repeated. "I'm going to kick his fucking ass. He treated you like shit after everything happened with Jonah. And it wasn't your fault."

I held up my hands, holding back tears. "I'm fine," I said, my voice cracking.

"That's it, now I'm going to kill him," Archer said, rolling up his sleeves.

"Please, stop. We're adults. We can handle this. Sure, it's a lot of emotions. And none of us knows exactly what happened during everything that went down. None of us talked about what happened. Hell, in this family, we do an excellent job of *not* talking about the fact that I'm a widow." They all went silent as they looked at me.

"Seriously. I lost my husband. Yes, he was my best friend, but he was my husband in the eyes of the law. That meant I had to go through the paperwork of death when it came to losing an eighteen-year-old to cystic fibrosis. I've dealt with that. I've dealt with my emotions, and I handled what I had to do with the rest of my life, trying to figure out how to grow up with part of the world watching me. I dealt with it. But we don't ever speak about it. And that's okay. We don't have to discuss my past in excruciating detail. But if *we* don't talk about it, you sure as hell know that Jacob and I have never talked about it. I don't know how he feels about me, really. I don't know exactly why he hates me, other than the fact that I took time with his brother away from him."

"Jonah wanted an escape," Benjamin said insightfully. "None of us were sure about you marrying a kid when you were a kid yourself, but we understood why you did it."

I flinched at that, but knew he was right. "I know nobody wanted me to marry him—other than his parents and Jonah. But I did. I wanted to make Jonah happy."

"And you did. He had happiness leading up to the wedding and the days you had left with him," Paige whispered. "And I'm sorry Jacob was hurt, but he doesn't get to treat you like shit."

"You're right. I told him he didn't get to, and we'll deal with it."

"Are you still going up to see his parents?" Beckett asked, his gaze on mine. I shrugged.

"Yes. I eat there almost every Sunday. And you know with Kelley being sick, I just need to be there for them."

"That's why Jacob moved here," Paige said, her eyes wide as it dawned on both of us.

"Damn," I whispered. "They never mentioned it to me."

"They've had a lot on their minds," Archer said, wincing.

"Or they didn't want to bother me with the fact that they knew their son hated me. Still does. It's fine. I'll deal with it. Jacob must be here to help his mom, and that is an admirable trait. He was always great for Jonah. So, yes, we will find a way to make it work. Now that it's out in the open, nobody needs to go and kick anyone's ass or castrate anyone."

"What's this about castration?"

I looked up at my father and groaned. "I swear, we need to close the door the next time we talk about this."

"Or we can just not talk about it ever again," Beckett said dryly.

I snorted. "Hi, Mom and Dad, come on in."

"I take it you're talking about something weird since your little assistant is out there hiding?" my dad said, and I grimaced.

"He's the assistant project manager," Beckett said through gritted teeth. "He's not my *little assistant*."

"Not that there's anything wrong with an assistant," Paige said. "But I prefer office manager."

"Because that's your title." I shook my head.

As Clay walked into the room, we all got to work. Montgomery Builders was now in session. Montgomery Inc. was down in Denver, along with Montgomery Ink. The one with the *K* was a tattoo shop that some of my Denver cousins ran. Another tattoo shop called Montgomery Ink Too was located in Colorado Springs. I figured once the next generation of Montgomerys aged, they would probably start popping up new Montgomery Inks and Incs all over the state and world. It would be nice. However, our family was none of that. We were Montgomery Builders, something that came from my dad's Montgomery side, not my mother's. When my parents got married, the family joke was that it was nice that my mother didn't have to bother changing her name. They were not blood-related or cousins, even fifth removed. At least from what they could tell. But the union was still rife with family tension. My father did not like his brothers-in-law—my uncles.

Therefore, he did not like that there was another construction company in the family. Montgomery Builders did not work with Montgomery Inc., and had nothing to do with my uncle—or now my cousins—who ran it.

And that was all due to my father. I loved the man, but he could be a righteous asshole sometimes. Okay, most of the time. And since he was currently taking over the meeting during this project, this was one of those times. Officially, my mother and father didn't have roles with Montgomery Builders. They oversaw everything we did and held the purse strings, but they'd handed the reins to us over time as we grew into our roles. We could have gone into any other field, but all of us had fallen in love with the family business and had followed our goals towards being part of it.

I was an architect and helped design every single project we worked on. Benjamin was our landscape architect and had a whole team for himself. Paige was our office manager and pretty much kept us running—and on our toes—while Archer, much to my father's dismay, was our lead plumber. Dad had wanted my brother to be an electrician or maybe an architect or something, but Archer wanted to be a plumber. And that was what he had ended up going to school for, and what he worked his ass off doing now. Beckett was our construction project manager and currently butting heads with my father on yet another item.

I pinched the bridge of my nose. "We've already decided what we're doing on this line item," I said. "Beckett's right."

Beckett gave me a tight nod, and I looked at my dad, trying not to wince. One did not argue with Russell Montgomery. But I was doing so. We were adults here, and my parents would simply have to learn to deal with their kids being in charge. Or back off. I hoped they'd retire soon, because we could not keep doing this.

Though I wasn't sure how we would get them to do that.

"I'm just saying. It would make more sense to do it this way." My father started outlining a whole new plan that would radically shift how we worked towards green materials and stayed on target. I shook my head. "No, we're trying to go into the new world. Global warming is an issue. We're trying not to build to the point where we hurt our ecosystem. Plus, we're in Colorado. We may not be in Boulder where they're completely crunchy granola, but those in Fort Collins can hold our own."

"I don't understand you Millennials," Dad grumbled.

"I think I might be a Xennial," Paige said, looking up from her notes.

I winced. "Not the time, Paige."

"That's true," she said, going back to her tablet.

"Fine, do it your way. But just remember, our name is on everything we do."

"We know," Beckett said, and Benjamin leaned back in his chair, shaking his head.

"This is a big project," my father repeated, and I rolled my shoulders back. "If we don't get this right, we're not getting bids for anything else in the city. If this is the project you want to put your new twist on within the operation, then it needs to be perfect. Any errors or mishaps will ruin the company and this family."

My mother nodded as if they weren't cutting down their children with their high expectations. We should have been used to it by now, but it still wasn't easy.

Our parents loved us. They just enjoyed the competition with my mother's siblings more. They wanted to do things their way, and while their way had made our family what it was, and was perfectly reasonable and sustainable, my siblings and I knew we needed to change a few things to help keep us healthy, relevant, and helpful.

And, deep down, I knew it wasn't the fact that we wanted to change things. No, it was the fact that my cousins down in Denver were doing the same things. We had all come together and decided to work towards a better future for our community and our families.

And my father wanted nothing to do with that or them.

"Okay, that's good for now," my mother said, tapping my dad's knee. He looked at her, gave a tight nod, and stood.

My mother loved her brothers, but she loved her husband more. So, she was constantly engaged in a tug of war between them. And while I understood, it was exhausting being in the middle, especially when you were a child and didn't want to be part of any of it at all.

Dad looked at each of us. "Okay, get it done. Montgomerys forever."

We nodded, though refrained from saying it back. The rest of the Montgomerys had a special tattoo, a family motto of sorts called the Montgomery Iris, a little M and I surrounded by a circle and flowers. My siblings and I had those tattoos in secret, mostly because if my father ever found out, he would probably disown us. The other cousins had gotten them, too, all taken care of and inked by one of the three tattoo artists in the family.

Mine was on my hip, where no one could see it unless I took off my bathing suit. And I would not be showing anyone that flesh anytime soon, thank you very much.

We had wanted to show solidarity with the whole set of Montgomerys, ignoring my dad's rage. Therefore, we did not say "Montgomerys forever," because we knew he wasn't talking about the other half of us.

It was such a strange way to live, but we were so used to it after all these years, it rarely even fazed us. However, my dad was right, this project *was* massive, and if we failed at it, we could put the business in the red. It was a different time for our company, and we understood it. All of us did. We worked hard to make sure that we were doing things the right way and safely. Though, sometimes, my dad made things a little more complicated.

Paige and Clay left with notes, Beckett trailing them as he went over what they were doing for the day. Archer smiled at me, waved, and then went off to his project site for the day. I looked down at my notes, knowing I needed to get some sketching in before I went to one of the sites. I looked up at Benjamin. He smiled at me, and I frowned.

"What?" I asked.

"I know today was your day to have the meeting in your office rather than in one of the main rooms, but I wanted to say we're going to be okay. We've got this."

We rotated where we had the meetings, ensuring that each of our offices ended up being the corporate head office at times, even if only in our heads. Sometimes, we met in the main meeting room, but we liked to change it up because it helped us creatively. At least, that's what we told ourselves. I just thought we liked moving around to annoy my dad—not that I would tell him that.

"We've got this," I said, standing up to hug him.

Benjamin kissed the top of my head and squeezed my shoulder. "And if you need us to castrate Jacob Queen, we will," he said, deadpan. I punched him in the gut, but considering my brother had an eight-pack, all it did was hurt my hand.

"Go dig something. That hurt."

"You shouldn't have hit me," he said lightheartedly and then strolled out of my office, leaving me with a smile on my face. Truthfully, after that morning, I honestly hadn't thought I would be able to. Likely, that's what Benjamin had wanted.

My family might be loud, rambunctious, and a little nosy, but I loved them more than anything.

CHAPTER 4

Jacob

From the outside, there hadn't been too many changes to the home I grew up in. The tall oak tree still stood in front of the house—though it seemed a bit taller to me. Flower beds lined the front, though those changed with the seasons as my mother loved to plant things that could outlast the Colorado winters. Mom and Dad had painted the door a bright, cheery red, a color that stood out amidst the rest of the exterior's dark gray and white tones. Some of the other neighbors had gone with similar concepts in colors they liked, and it always brought a slight smile to my face. The idea that my parents had been able to not move on per se, but find strength, made me feel as if we'd done something right. They were living in the now, rather than wallowing in what we had all lost so many years ago.

I'd been to this home numerous times since I moved away

for college. I spent holidays here, although I never stayed overnight. It had always been easier for me to drive the hour or so back down south to my home.

Now, I was closer because my parents needed me, and it was about time they let someone help and take care of them.

I pulled in next to an unfamiliar car and frowned. I didn't think anyone would be here tonight for our family dinner, but maybe I was wrong. Or perhaps it was only a neighbor visiting before they left for the evening. Either way, if it made my mother smile to have company, that was all that mattered. She needed smiles more than ever these days —Dad, too.

I got out of the car and grabbed the bouquet of wild-flowers I'd brought. My mother loved fresh bouquets, even if some didn't last more than a few days in water. She loved the blooms, and I would do anything to keep her blooming right along with them.

I went to the front door and let myself in. My mother wasn't up to running towards the door these days, and I didn't want to bother Dad when he could be busy.

"Honey, I'm home," I said, keeping my voice light. They didn't need to know that I'd had a tough case today, and my temples pulsed with stress. They didn't need to know that I had moved in next door to the girl they loved—one I couldn't stand. Or maybe she was just the person I told myself I couldn't stand so I didn't have to deal with the fact that I'd lost my baby brother.

I quickly pushed those thoughts away because they didn't matter. I was only letting my shrink's words slide into my brain, and they were muddying everything up.

I knew what Annabelle had done, and there was no changing that.

"We're back here, son," Dad called from the sunroom. I slipped off my shoes before making my way inside, looking around at the changes from when I had lived here. There were more open spaces now, places where my mother's wheelchair needed to move, and though the house was one story, most everything was up in the front where my parents' master bedroom was located. They had the sunroom in the back, but they rarely used it, at least from what I remembered.

Maybe Mom was having a better day and they wanted to use the space. I sure as hell hoped so.

As I moved into the back, I frowned, recognizing the woman kneeling by my mother. Annabelle Montgomery was next to my mother's chair, smiling softly as she patted my mom's hands, and the two of them shared a conspiratorial laugh.

My hands clenched, the flowers' stems crushing in my grip. I forced myself to take a deep breath and let it out slowly, releasing my hold.

"Oh, Jacob, you're here," Mom said, beaming up at me.

She looked gorgeous, even though she had lost half her weight over the past few years. She'd had diminished function in her legs first, and now, she was losing mobility in her hands. She was having a more challenging time keeping her head up these days, too, and leaned against the chair's headrest more often than not.

She was my mother and looked exactly like the woman who had raised Jonah and me, yet she also looked like a stranger. It wasn't fair. Mom had been through enough. My father had been through enough. I hated that he had to watch her slowly lose her freedom, just like we'd had to do with Jonah.

"I didn't know we'd be having company," I said through gritted teeth, though I tried to keep a smile on my face.

My mother's eyes widened and then narrowed as Annabelle stood up and smoothed down her dress.

"Hello, Jacob. Your mother and I were just commenting on the fact that you moved into my neighborhood."

"We told you, son, it's a good development," my father said, handing me a beer as he passed.

I looked down and scowled. "So you knew the Montgomerys built it?" I asked, trying to keep the derision out of my tone.

Annabelle raised her chin, and my mother gave me a speaking look.

"We wanted you to have the best. The Montgomerys do the best. I didn't know you'd be moving next door to Annabelle, though, since it's not like I know every street number up there. However, I'm glad you'll be close. In case she needs to take care of a spider or something," Mom said, winking over at Annabelle.

The woman I wasn't sure what to make of rolled her eyes. "I can take care of spiders on my own."

"Really?" I asked dryly.

Annabelle squared her shoulders. "Of course, I set them free. They help eat the other bugs that I hate. But we're in Colorado. There are trees everywhere. There are going to be bugs. And don't worry, I have many brothers and cousins who can help me if needed. You don't need to worry your pretty little head."

I ignored the tone, even as my mother grinned at it.

Well, it seemed I knew whose side she was on. Not that she was supposed to know there were sides at all.

"I'm just glad you're back in town," Mom said softly.

Putting all thoughts of her from my mind, I moved forward, dropping to one knee in front of the woman I loved more than anything.

"I'm glad I'm back, too," I whispered and handed her the flowers, making sure to rest them on her lap so she didn't have to grip them.

She smiled at me, her eyes a little watery, and I reached out and rubbed my thumb across her cheek, brushing away a tear.

"They're lovely, Jacob."

"As are you," I teased.

"You're such a charmer. I have no idea why you aren't married yet."

"I have a few ideas," Annabelle mumbled under her breath, and my mother's eyes twinkled with laughter.

My dad coughed into his beer and then shook his head. "You know, I like her. And, Jacob? You do have a sly tongue. You're nice and sweet to your mom, but I'm pretty sure you get all lawyered out when it comes to dating."

I scowled, standing up. "What does that even mean? And how did I become the center of this? Besides, we're not talking about dating. I moved here to be with you guys. Dating isn't in the picture."

My mom looked as if she were about to shake her head but instead leaned against the headrest of her chair. I hated that she was in pain and there was nothing I could do about it. If I talked about it or focused on it, she would only become embarrassed and agitated. Still, I risked a glance at my father, who shook his head gently. Dad was watching her, and my mom would say something if she needed help. I just had to get used to seeing my mother this way. As if that would ever happen.

"It would be nice if you settled down," Mom said.

I smiled, ice coating my veins because the unsaid words scared me to death.

It would be nice if I could settle down...before she was gone.

Jesus Christ. How was my dad doing this? How was I supposed to help?

Instead of wallowing, I winked and gave them the smirk I had practiced when I was a teen. "I'll settle down once I find who I want. Before that, though, I have to taste the wares."

Annabelle scoffed, while my mother rolled her eyes, and my dad laughed. "I raised you better than that," Mom said.

"Maybe, but I like watching Annabelle's color deepen into a plum red as I keep speaking."

"Oh, I'm not angry," Annabelle corrected. "I just feel pity for you. I mean, all those women out there rejecting you left and right? It's got to be hard."

"Nice," I said through my teeth.

"You did ask for it, son," Dad said. "Okay, dinner is ready. Let's head into the dining room and see what we have to eat."

"Are you sure it's okay that I'm here?" Annabelle asked, wringing her hands in front of herself for a bare instant before she noticed me watching. Immediately, she very deliberately placed her hands on either side of her and looked as if she weren't worried at all.

She should be worried. I hated that she was here, reminding me of everything I had lost, and being in the way. Why couldn't she just go back to her family and stop trying to impede on mine?

"Of course. You're family," Mom said, her fingers twitching.

Annabelle immediately reached out to clasp my mother's hands, giving them a slight squeeze. "That's a lovely thing to say. And I'm pretty sure that Roger mentioned something about lemon chicken?"

"World-famous," Dad said. I ignored the lines of strain at the corners of his eyes. He was exhausted, and I knew that while we were waiting for insurance to cover the full-time nurse, Dad was in limbo, like Mom was. I helped as much as I could, but between work and the fact that my parents didn't want me doing everything, it wasn't easy. But tonight wasn't about that. Tonight was about happiness and peace—even if Annabelle Montgomery was a part of it.

We settled into the dining room and ate a lovely dinner. Mom smiled and chatted the entire time. She wanted us to be together as a family, apparently even if a Montgomery was part of that. As we cleaned up, Dad took Mom back to their bedroom to help with her next set of meds, and I did dishes as Annabelle dried.

"I didn't realize you would be here," Annabelle whispered.

I looked over my shoulder, grateful that with the layout of the house, Mom and Dad wouldn't be able to hear. "I thought we were going to stay out of each other's way."

She shook her head, taking a plate from me. "I tried. But I have a standing dinner with your parents on Sundays. And sometimes I see them more often. Now that you're here, it seems you'll be a part of that. I've done this for years, Jacob. I'm not just now swooping in to ruin your life." She paused. "According to you, I already did that years ago."

I flinched but ignored the barb. I was an asshole, and I knew it. "I don't understand," I growled.

"You don't need to understand it. My relationship with your parents and your brother has nothing to do with you."

"That's where you're wrong. It has everything to do with me."

"You're acting like such an idiot," she spat.

"I'm acting like a man who watched you parade around on TV after my brother died. I watched you in a pretty wedding dress, soaking up the limelight for apparent funds or whatever. Money my parents never mentioned to me. That is what I see when I look at you. I don't see the good girl my parents apparently do. You can take this precious little fantasy of yours and shove it. I will not let you hurt my mom and dad."

Annabelle stared at me, blinking slowly before quietly setting down the plate she held, her hands shaking. "Please tell your parents thank you for dinner. I need to go."

I cursed under my breath. "Annabelle—"

"No. I think you've said enough." Then she turned and walked out of the kitchen. I sighed.

"You're going to want to come into the living room, son," my father said, his voice stony.

I set down the plate I had been washing, shut off the water, and turned to see my father glaring from the other end of the kitchen, his hands fisted at his sides.

"Dad—" I began.

"No. You're going to get your ass out into the living room, and we're going to have a talk. Because if I don't have a second to calm down as you walk in here, I'm going to beat your ass for the way you just talked to that young lady."

"You don't know what she's done."

"No, it seems that *you* don't. So, get your fucking ass into the living room."

I hadn't seen my dad with this much energy or spark in months. I blinked at him before exhaling, then turned on my heel and made my way to the living room as ordered.

My dad came the other way, his chest heaving as he

worked through whatever the hell he was thinking. My mom glared at me, her mouth pressed into a thin line. "How could you?" she asked, her voice soft, cracking.

"What? What is it about her? You saw what the press did with her. She used it for personal gain. I don't know what kind of game she was playing, maybe looking for sponsorship deals or money or speaking deals. I don't know. But her face was plastered everywhere, the perfect little wife who gave up her innocence for my brother. It was a circus around here at the end. Don't you remember?"

My mother swallowed hard. My dad paced behind her before gently putting his hands on her shoulders.

"Annabelle Montgomery is our daughter-in-law," my dad bit out, and I let out a breath.

"Maybe legally, but not in any other way."

"You do not get to put your titles on her."

I looked at my mother as she spoke but didn't say anything. I had a feeling if I did, I would only dig myself in deeper. I didn't understand why they defended her like this or what I could be missing.

"I thought you knew everything, but it seems you were so blinded by grief or anger or whatever the hell you think she did, that you missed some key aspects of what happened in those final moments. So, we're going to tell you," my mother said.

"What the hell are you talking about?" I asked, uneasy.

My dad patted my mother's shoulder and then leaned down. "You rest, I'll explain," Dad said. He looked up at me, grief weighing heavily on his face. "When we knew Jonah wouldn't have long, when we knew we were nearing the end, he said that he wanted one last thing. A hail Mary, he called it. He wanted to marry his best friend, to call her his bride, something he would never be able to do thanks to the disease riding his body."

"I know that part," I whispered.

"But do you know that Annabelle didn't want to marry him or have any part of it? That she was afraid it would be too much for him?"

I shook my head, frowning. "No, I thought she egged him on."

"You're such an idiot," my dad said, and my head shot up.

"I know what I saw."

"You saw what she wanted you to see, the brave face she put on because she was losing her best friend. And she could have used another friend then, but you turned away from her because you were scared. And I get it. We did, too." My dad let out a shaky breath, his eyes filling with tears. "We knew it was insane. That not everybody would understand. But it's what he wanted, and when Annabelle saw your brother looking so happy at the thought of a wedding and some form of normalcy, she said yes. And she let herself become this other person who had to deal with the media and everything else because she needed to breathe. I only know a fraction of what she felt," my father added.

"She wrapped herself in such a shell that we couldn't break through. But she was strong for Jonah. For our son. Your brother. And she raised thousands of dollars for research for cystic fibrosis. Hundreds of thousands. She went viral before viral was a thing. She did the media coverage and everything because she couldn't do anything else to help the boy she loved. So, yes, she became a minor local celebrity and a small spark on the national media circuit along with Jonah. And I still don't know all of the emotions she experienced, but I do know that she didn't want to do it. Maybe she hated every minute of it. Perhaps she didn't mind it. Who are we to judge either way?"

"She said you asked her," I whispered, trying to reconcile what I had felt before and what was going on now.

"Yes," my mother said, her voice firm.

"Why?" I asked.

"Because Jonah wanted it. My baby boy was dying, and I needed to give him something. So we asked Annabelle to do something she didn't really want to do because I didn't know what else we had for him," my mother whispered. "And, yes, it was only a marriage in name and on paper, but it gave him joy for a few days." Tears ran down my mother's face, and I reached out to wipe them away, but my father shook his head and took care of her. I felt the blow even though it never actually came.

"I don't know what to think," I whispered.

"All I know is that life is short, and we have learned the hard way that we don't get to decide when the end comes," my mother said, her voice stern. This time, tears slid down *my* cheeks.

"We don't know what happens after this, but we do know what we can accomplish in the life we have. Who we can be during the *time* we have. So, I need you to go to Annabelle and fix this. I need you to see who she was so you can find out who she became. Because I love that little girl like she's my daughter. She gave my son peace in a time there was none. And for that, I will forever be grateful. And I need you to know that we love you, too. I know you're grieving, but I didn't realize you didn't know the full truth. That we asked. And that she hated every bit of it but was willing to do it because she loved Jonah. I need you to know that. And I need you to fix this."

My mother leaned back in her wheelchair, exhausted. I stood there, my hands shaking.

"I didn't know," I whispered.

Dad sighed. "Clearly. Now, fix this. Figure it out. Because she's not the monster you made her out to be."

"Then am I the monster?" I asked.

"The only monster here is fate," my mother said softly. "But we learned that a long time ago." And then she leaned against the headrest and closed her eyes. I could tell she wanted privacy, and my dad needed to help her.

I nodded tightly and met my father's gaze before turning on my heel and leaving. I needed to fix this. If not for Jonah, then for my parents. Because I'd said I would do anything for them. Maybe getting my head out of my ass was the first step.

CHAPTER 5

Annabelle

I had already called him a dumb son of a bitch. I didn't know what else to say. Because I couldn't hate him, I couldn't yell and thrash and be angry anymore.

I didn't know what to feel. Jacob hated me so much. The man I had called a friend, who had laughed with me, cried with me, and had been in my life just as much as Jonah before everything changed, was someone I didn't recognize anymore. Only it had been over six years now, and people did change. Maybe. Perhaps they did. Though it was possible I hadn't known Jacob at all.

I hiccupped a sob, annoyed with myself for crying. I shouldn't be weeping. It wasn't my place to be emotional over this. I needed to get over whatever was going on in my brain and focus on the important stuff. My family, my work, and I guessed, my soul.

Screw Jacob Queen.

Even if he was hurting.

Even if he hated me.

I turned into my driveway, not bothering to pull into the garage. I had a bunch of boxes in the way since I was rearranging a few things in my home office. That meant I got to park on the driveway, where I'd rather not.

I got out of the car, telling myself I would have a cup of evening coffee and work on my project. Dad was counting on us. The whole family was. And that meant I needed to do my part. I had to get my mind out of the past and stop worrying about what others thought about me. And, yes, that meant I needed to stop fretting about how my father felt about me—but that was a whole other kettle of fish.

"Hey, you're home early," a voice said from my left. I turned, steeling myself.

I pasted a smile on my face. Not because I didn't like the man speaking but because I didn't want to talk to anyone. Hotch was my other neighbor, and while he was kind, he was a little insistent that I go out with him. Maybe he felt like we were closer friends than I did.

I wasn't a hundred percent sure what he wanted from me. I knew I needed to tell him straight out that it would never happen between us, but I had already tried that, and he'd simply waved it off and said he was only being neighborly. Said he hadn't meant it like it may have sounded or how I'd interpreted his words.

I wasn't sure if I believed him. But in the end, it didn't matter. He hadn't bothered me about it again, but he was a little persistent with wanting to be a part of my life, even when I wasn't sure what I wanted.

Then the meaning of his words truly hit me, and I frowned.

"What do you mean?" I asked Hotch as he sauntered up, a pleasant smile on his face, his hair slicked back perfectly. He looked like a run-of-the-mill neighbor without a care in the world. One who worked hard at his job and his health. He was average-looking, friendly...and didn't do a thing for me.

I really wasn't in the mood to deal with men right now.

"It's Sunday. I figured you were off at that dinner you go to."

"You know that?" I asked, drawing out my words.

His eyes widened as if he realized that he was acting peculiarly, but he quickly shook his head. "I'm sorry. You mentioned once that you were going out to dinner, and I noticed that you leave at the same time every Sunday. I like schedules and things like that. You know me, I have planners about planners."

I nodded, not moving forward. "Oh. Well, dinner was fine." *A lie.*

"Are you sure? You look sad. Do you want to talk about it? We can get some coffee. Just you and me."

I shook my head, keeping the smile on my face. "No, I want to go inside. But thank you for checking in on me."

"No problem. Anytime you want coffee, I'm your man."

"I'm sure," I said, not delving into what he was really asking. Still, I gave him a little wave and made my way into the house, locking the door behind me. I looked at him through the blinds and saw him walk back to his car, the one he had been washing when I came up.

He wasn't creepy, just a guy who liked to ask me out often. Or like any suburban cul-de-sac neighbor, happened to know my schedule. I mean, I knew when he went to work, and the fact that he had guys' night every Thursday. I guessed it wasn't too strange, but coming from Jacob attacking me as he had, I was a little raw and over dealing with human beings.

I went to make coffee. As I finished, the doorbell rang. I cursed under my breath. I was not in the mood to deal with Hotch again. Sure, he was nice, but sometimes he clearly didn't get the hint. I looked through the peephole and wanted to bang my head against the door. If only it *had* been Hotch. Perhaps I should have gone out for coffee with him. Hotch was pleasant and not threatening at all. He didn't make me feel like crap. He didn't make me feel anything, and that was the problem.

"Annabelle, I know you're in there. I see your car."

"Go away, Jacob," I called through the door.

"I'm here to apologize. To say I'm an asshole. I can shout it through the door, but we already talked about how we don't want the cops making a visit to the cul-de-sac."

I groaned and knew that I needed to get this over with. Plus, Jacob mentioned apologizing. I knew his mother probably forced him into it, but if we did this, maybe we could get it over with.

And I wouldn't have to feel like crap anymore.

I sucked in a deep breath, rolled my shoulders back, and steeled myself as I opened the door. "Mr. Queen," I said, glaring at him.

His lips quirked for a moment. "Only people on the other side of the bench call me that," Jacob teased.

"I bet they think you're just as much of an asshole as I do." So much for trying to play nice.

"I deserve that when it comes to you." He paused. "May I come in? I mean, I don't mind airing my dirty laundry out in the middle of the street, but your neighbor's out here glaring at me with a hose in his hand. And by the look on his face, I'm not sure he'll stop at merely spraying me down."

"Come on in. Though you should know, I'm not in the mood to air anything right now." I stepped back, and he walked into my home, his hands in his pockets. He was clearly doing his best to look non-threatening, as if he hadn't already tried to rip out my heart and stomp on it a few dozen times.

"Make it quick. I need to get to work."

He gave me a curious look. "It's Sunday..."

"You're a lawyer opening up a practice here. I'm pretty sure you should be working right now, too. Let's not get into who's working too much."

"You're right. I should be working. However, I'm not yet because I'm an asshole, and I needed to make sure you knew that."

"You don't need to explain that to me. Your actions spoke far louder than your words ever could. Now, if that's all, you can go home. I think you know the way."

"Annabelle—" Jacob began.

"What?" I snapped, not liking how he said my name. I didn't know what it meant, and I definitely did not want to think about the reasons it could mean something.

Ever.

"I'm sorry."

"For what? You're supposed to be good with words. And I know that people who say they're sorry but don't say what they're sorry about only want to get through the apology quicker. So, you should tell me exactly what you mean."

"I'm sorry. I'm sorry for what I thought before. How I treated you. And how I'm treating you now. I'm finally listening to what you said, and what my parents said all along." He pulled his hands out of his pockets, then ran one over his face. "I miss him so fucking much, Annabelle."

A little part of me broke, and I swallowed the lump in my throat. "I miss him, too, Jacob. The two of us continuing to fight won't bring him back, though."

"I know," he said, dropping his hand. "I felt like I was losing him before he was even gone when we were younger. And I know now that he was just scared. But I needed someone to blame, and everyone else blamed God, so I blamed you."

I wiped a tear from my face, annoyed that I was even crying. "I blamed God for a while, too. Then I blamed the doctors and fate. And then myself for not finding a way to cure him when I was eighteen and had no idea what I was doing."

Jacob's eyes widened. "Seriously?"

"Of course. It's all stages. But the thing was, I never blamed you for walking away. For looking at me the way you did because I thought you were hurting."

He pressed his lips together and gave me a tight nod. "You were the easiest scapegoat. And I saw what was happening and took that twisted narrative and made it true, rather than leaving it as the fiction it was."

"I hated every minute of the charade. The press. I had to put on the fake smiles because the world needed to see we were brave, and that I wasn't dying inside. But we raised so much money for research. And there have been a few break-throughs since. Small ones, but it's something."

"I know," he whispered. "I keep up on it. And a percentage of my income goes to it. That and research for ALS."

I pressed my lips together, trying to keep my composure.

"I'm so sorry about Kelley. I love her so much. It's not fair that she's sick."

"It's not fair what's happened to my family at all. But you've always been here, and I never knew. It's like my parents decided to make sure that I never knew how much you took care of them. How wonderful you are to them."

"I think they remembered how you felt about me and didn't want to make things more awkward."

"Until I needed to move back because my mom was running out of time. And she's right. There isn't enough time in the world for me to continue hating you. Especially when you don't deserve it."

I let out a breath, shaking my head. "That's the oddest apology I've ever heard."

"It was the strangest reason to hate someone I've ever heard," Jacob grumbled. "It's going to take me a while to untwist the narrative I created in my head. But I'm telling you now, I'm sorry. I'm sorry for what I said, and for what I thought. I'll figure out how to deal with this."

"We live next door to each other, Jacob. And I'm not leaving your parents' lives. Especially now. We're going to see each other often. Can you handle that?"

He gave me a tight nod. "I think it's time I figure out exactly who Annabelle Montgomery is."

I shook my head. "I'm the same person I always was."

"Now that's a lie," Jacob corrected. "And I think that maybe we should get to know the people we are now, rather than dwelling on the people we left behind in the shadows."

I looked at him then, wondering what I felt. Was it warmth? I didn't know. But I wanted to reach out and hold him, tell him that everything would be all right, even though that was a lie. I didn't like that I noticed how his eyes darkened, the way his lips parted. I didn't like that we were buried in memories of a time gone by and mired in loss and fractured silences. And yet all I could do was look at him and wonder who this man was. Who *was* Jacob Queen?

Betrayal slid over me then, and I knew it made no sense. It wasn't as if Jonah and I had genuinely been in love. Not like that. And yet, this was Jacob. I shouldn't feel anything. Especially not right now.

Still, I had to say the words. "I would like to get to know you," I whispered.

He studied my face for a long moment before he finally spoke. "Good. Because I think we should. Mom and Dad love you so much. I'd like to get to know that woman. And I don't want you to carry the burden of my family alone any longer."

I shook my head. "You were always there. Even if you weren't in the same room."

"Maybe, but I'm here full-time now. Let's help them together if you want to. Or you can step away so you can breathe. You don't have to bear any responsibility."

I shook my head. "I will always be a part of their lives, of our old life, who we were. And that means I'm going to be a traveler on this road your family takes. So, I guess we're in this together."

"Then I suppose I should start with this." He held out his hand. "Hello, I'm Jacob Queen. Permanent asshole and perpetual insomniac workaholic."

My lips twitched. "Hello," I said, sliding my hand into his, ignoring the heat between us. "I'm Annabelle Montgomery. Also a workaholic, a slight insomniac, and someone who loves her family very much."

His lips softened into a smile, and then he let my hand go.

I ignored the fact that it felt chilled now without his heat. "It's nice to meet you, Annabelle."

"You, as well, Jacob."

"I don't think I ever really hated you," he admitted.

"I think I was starting to hate you," I replied, and he laughed.

"I wouldn't blame you. It's going to take me a little while to fix things in my head, but let's be friends until then."

"I don't know about friends," I said honestly. "Maybe neighbors?"

He snorted. "Neighbors, I can do. Now, I'm going to let you have your peace because I haven't let you have that for most of the night. Just know if you need me to crawl over gravel, I can do that. I do have a deposition tomorrow, though, so I may have to work around that."

I laughed, surprising myself, and shook my head. "No need to flay yourself. I know you miss your brother. And I know you needed someone to hate. Just don't let it be me anymore."

He met my gaze, and once again, I ignored the little ping I felt that warned me something was different.

"I don't think I can ever hate you again, Annabelle Montgomery."

Before I could say anything, he turned on his heel and left, and I had to wonder what the hell had happened.

CHAPTER 6

Jacob

"I need you to get me the deposition in the next hour," I said to my assistant. He nodded, quickly typing on his tablet. I looked at my other assistant, who also nodded as she slid a hand over her dark hair. It had been a long day, and the amount of paperwork—even for lawyers— was insane. It would be a long night unless we figured out our plan now.

"You've got it, Mr. Queen," Dustin said.

"You also have a meeting at seven," Seressia said, frowning. "You have meetings back to back tomorrow."

"Understood. It'll be busier than usual tomorrow because I need to take Friday off," I said, and they both knew why. Mom had a doctor's appointment and I planned to be with her and my father. We were structuring my practice the way

I needed to, and we'd find a way to make it work, even if it killed me.

"You have court on Thursday, but you should be fine for that," Dustin said, looking down at his tablet again.

My lips quirked. "I hope so. It is kind of my job."

"Well, you did bring us up from Denver to this…whatever town you think this is," Seressia said, looking out the window at the barren landscape behind me.

I snorted. "It only looks like that because this window faces east rather than the mountains. I gave the conference room the mountain view."

"You're the boss, you should have the mountain view."

"No, because then I would never get any work done. We're doing okay, you guys. Right?"

They both nodded. "Okay, let's get this done. Maybe you can be out of here before six." I knew they wanted to roll their eyes at me, but they didn't. Instead, they gave me tight nods before getting back to work. Sadly, it would probably be more like eight, and they'd be taking work home right along with me. I needed another staff member on the books, and we were working on it. Unfortunately, it was a little slow-going. Mostly because two of the other staff members I wanted to bring up with me from Denver were on maternity leave. Their babies were cute, and I was very happy for my staff, but I sure as hell missed them right now.

I made a note to check in on both of them, not to ask them when they were coming back but because I was honestly interested and cared. I was trying to be a better boss. Attempting to be a better person. And I could do that even if I felt like I had no idea what I was doing.

That only reminded me that I was failing even worse at life and choices when it came to Annabelle. I had been such a fucking asshole. I needed to work on who I was and determine why I had acted the way I did. She seemed to take it with grace, but I had a feeling that was just Annabelle, and had nothing to do with my apology.

I'd be seeing her soon. Not that we had anything planned, but she would be at my parents' house the next time they had a big family dinner, *and* she lived next door to me. There was no escaping that, even though I was pretty sure she worked as many long hours as I did, and both of us were rarely home.

I pushed Annabelle and that weird moment between us the last time I had spoken to her out of my mind. I did not need to think about the heat or awareness I'd felt. I had simply been exhausted and losing my mind a little. I wasn't thinking anything else when it came to her. I let out a breath, pinched the bridge of my nose, and forced myself to focus.

I worked for another couple of hours, Dustin having to bring me lunch when I lost track of time. I smiled my thanks, and he pointed to his eyes and then at the sandwich. I snorted.

"I'll eat it. Thank you for taking care of me."

"Somebody has to. You sure don't do it yourself." He spun on his heel and walked out, and I snorted.

I liked the duo. Seressia and Dustin. They worked well together, and they kept me on my toes. They pretty much ran the office. That meant that once we finished filling our staff and settled in a bit, eventually making more money for the practice, they would get raises. I wouldn't work them to death and not pay them. Nor would I work them to death. I hadn't liked that when I was just starting out, and even though I was young to have my own practice, I didn't want to be *that* boss. The one everybody feared and who forced them into heart attacks at the age of forty because they worked too hard, drank harder, and forgot about the real world. I also liked my paralegal, Lucas, who was currently researching for me. He worked as many hours, if not more, than I did. Lucas was probably buried in a book right now, and I didn't mind.

I opened the sandwich and looked over some briefs as my phone rang. Since it was the office phone, Dustin must have sent it back. I answered.

"Jacob Queen's office."

"Hello there, darling," my mother said. I smiled, leaning back in my chair.

I took a bite of the sandwich and grinned. "Hello."

"You're talking with your mouth full."

I winced. "Sorry, I figured since you called, I could take a break."

"That's good timing, then. Since you're eating, I don't have to nag you about that."

"I take care of myself."

"No, Dustin and Seressia take care of you, which is good. They know exactly how to make sure you don't work yourself into the ground. I just wanted to check on you." There was an awkward pause, and I cleared my throat and set my partially eaten sandwich down on the desk.

"I apologized to Annabelle. Told her I was a jerk and said I would work to do better. I am sorry, Mom."

I heard the relieved breath, and I winced.

"That's good to hear," she whispered. "She needs love, too. And so do you."

I shook my head and bit into the sandwich again so I wouldn't say what was on my mind.

"All I'm saying is that she could use a friend," my mother backpedaled. I rolled my eyes, though she couldn't see me.

"Sure. Whatever you say. I think Annabelle and I are going to try to be friends. Or at least nice neighbors."

"That's all I can ask. I could ask for much more, but I'll stick with that."

I shook my head again, even though, once more, she couldn't see me. "Thank you for checking in. That is why you called, right?"

"I just wanted to hear your voice." There was another pause, and my sandwich tasted like sawdust all of a sudden. I swallowed the last of the bite and wiped my hands on the napkin Dustin had given me.

"I'm glad you called. Call anytime—even if I'm in court. I'll take it."

"I will not call when you're not on a break."

"And how will you know that?"

"I have spies."

"Dustin and Seressia call you to let you know when I'm eating so you can call me?" I guessed.

"Maybe. And when your brilliant women get back to the office, they'll make sure I can take care of you, as well. I'm doing my best to make sure that all of the moms in that lovely little office of yours are taking care of their kids. You might be adults, but you'll always be our babies."

I let out a breath and tried not to focus on the fact that my heart broke a little inside. I needed to focus on the now and not what could happen in the future. "I love you, Mom."

"I love you, too, baby. Now you go put those criminals behind bars."

"That's not the type of law I'm working on up here," I said dryly.

"Maybe not, but you're still doing good work. You're brilliant. And I'm proud of you. Now, go do whatever paperwork you need to do."

I laughed. "That sounds about right."

We said our goodbyes and hung up, and I looked down at my desk, wondering what I would do when she didn't call on my lunches anymore. It wouldn't serve me to focus on that, but I'd moved up to Fort Collins and changed my entire life and career to be near my family. And after she was gone? After the doctors were finally proven right?

I'd stay, wouldn't I? Or would I run again? I shoved those thoughts from my mind, not wanting to focus on them. It would only make me ill again, and I couldn't breathe if I let my thoughts go down a path of shadows so far in the future —at least I hoped it was far in the future.

I cleaned up my desk, pulled out my water, drank half of it down, and then got back to work. I'd focus on the paperwork in front of me, on the people who needed me right now, and then deal with everything else later.

There was a light tap on the door, and I looked up to see Seressia frowning at me.

"What?"

"There's someone here to speak to you. I wasn't sure if I should send them away or not."

For some strange reason, Annabelle's face popped into my mind, and I stood up. "Tall, average height, dark brown hair, vivid blue eyes?"

Seressia's smile made her look like a cat in cream, and I could have cursed. "No, but after work, once I'm not on the clock, I do believe you need to explain that to me."

I held back a wince. Damn it. Seressia was far too good at

ferreting out information, and I'd walked right into it. "No, I don't believe I do."

"Whatever you say. But, no, it's not her...whoever the dream girl is."

"Seressia."

She sighed and then visibly braced herself. "It's Mrs. Queen."

I closed my eyes, counted to five because I sure as hell wasn't going to make it to ten, and let out a breath. "Why don't you just send her back? I'm sure she didn't give you a reason for being here."

She gave me a pointed look. "Okay, we'll be here to call you out on business in ten minutes."

I snorted. "You know what, I'll take you up on that offer."

"It's what we're here for."

Seressia left, and a few moments later, I heard the click of heels against the hardwood of the older home we'd converted into my office.

Susan Queen was gorgeous. Vivid red hair and curls that framed her face. Her green eyes were piercing, and you never forgot them. She had a pointed chin and a semi-pointed nose. Her face was dusted with freckles, and she looked like a fey queen. She had sinful curves, something she called them herself, and looked as if she could take on the world.

And she did.

She had taken me on, after all—and then spat me out after she chewed on me a bit.

"Hello, Jacob. It's good to see you," she said softly as she made her way inside. She leaned forward, grabbed my shoulders, and air-kissed my cheek before leaning back to study my face.

"You look tired. How is Kelley?"

"Mother's doing just fine. Father, too. And I'm probably tired because it's the middle of a workday and I haven't had coffee since nine."

"Why don't we take care of that? I'll take you out for a cup. There has to be a little café around here. One owned by a little barista with a cute smile. Maybe one that serves the best cinnamon rolls in the state."

"How many Hallmark movies have you been watching lately?" I asked wryly.

"Enough. They're on Lifetime now, too. Though those are a little spicier."

"I don't have time for coffee, Susan."

She looked past me to the papers on my desk and frowned. "I'd hoped that you coming up here to this little town of yours would help you not work so much. I can see that isn't the case."

I resisted the urge to shove her out of my office because that wouldn't be nice. And I didn't hate Susan. I just didn't like her anymore. "Susan, first off, Fort Collins is not a little town. It's a city. A decent-sized one."

"It's not Denver."

"No, it's not. But it's my hometown and the place I'm living for the time being. Maybe forever," I added when her eyes brightened at the phrase *time being*.

"Well, let me take you out for that coffee."

"I'm busy, Susan. Why did you drive up here? It's over an hour out of your way."

She waved her hand. "I have business in Cheyenne tomorrow. A potential story. I decided to visit here first. See what you were up to."

"And you're staying the night in Cheyenne?" I asked.

"Bob has a hotel for us."

"You and Bob still seeing each other, then?" I asked, not sure why I even brought it up.

She gave me a look that spoke volumes. "No, but we still work together. There are two rooms in that hotel, thank you very much. However, I'm sure I could arrange to stay here for the night if you were accommodating."

I gritted my teeth. "No. There's no room at the inn for you, Susan."

"Pity." She let out a breath and looked up at me with wide eyes. I used to love staring into those eyes, the jade green color so intoxicating.

Now, I only saw all the lies.

"I am sorry," she whispered.

"You said it before."

"Well, I am. And maybe one day you'll believe me. I'm glad that you're here, settling down. Finding peace. You've needed it."

"Susan," I warned.

She held up a hand and shook her head. "I know. Can't touch the heart that is Jacob Queen. That was always the problem."

"We both know that wasn't the only problem."

"Perhaps. However, I am glad you're here. But I miss you."

I shook my head as warning bells sounded in my brain. "Okay, go get in the car and drive up with Bob to Cheyenne. You probably left him out there, didn't you?"

"He has an audiobook. And the man is monotonous. Not Bob," she said as my lips quirked. "The narrator. He has no inflection, but Bob's happy with it, so I'm dealing with it. However, I wanted to see you."

"You came, you saw, now it's time for you to go."

She looked at me then, studied my face and shrugged. "Be safe, Jacob."

And then my ex-wife walked out of my office. I let my head fall back. Today was a shitty day already, and, honestly, I only had myself to blame for the choices I'd made that led me to this point.

"That seemed fast enough. I didn't have to get you out for a meeting," Seressia said, and I growled.

"We're all out at six. I don't care what we're working on. We'll come back to it tomorrow. I'm pretty sure I'm going to need a drink, and me thinking about it here isn't going to cut it."

Seressia grinned as Dustin and Lucas laughed behind her. "You've got it, boss."

They left my office, and I went back to work, trying my best to focus on what I needed to do, rather than the outside world continually trying to drag me back in.

I didn't love Susan anymore. I hadn't for a long time. We'd been married for all of two years, and she'd cheated on me in the end. She and Bob had been happy for a split second, though apparently, they weren't anymore.

Susan had once called me too raw, too angry at life. Said she needed normalcy. Fort Collins would be too ordinary for her. I didn't know why she had come here, other than to disrupt my life because she didn't know how to settle herself. Either way, we were two flames that burned too brightly near each other. We didn't need to be in the same room anymore.

Being combustible meant leaving debris in your path, not a warm and bright glow.

And now, I was getting all poetic about my ex-wife. Time to get to work and focus on what was important. Not my future plans, not my ex-wife, and not a woman with blue eyes who kept haunting my daydreams.

By the time six p.m. rolled around, I was exhausted and really wanted to take off my tie and call it a day. I was true to my word and shoved my staff out the door before they had a chance to complain about it. They worked just as hard as I did, hence why they had disrupted their lives to come up here with me to begin with.

I had a feeling that Lucas and maybe Seressia would head back to Denver after they got a couple of additional years under their belts here and gained experience, but they were here for now, and we had an odd little work-family dynamic.

I looked down at my phone and figured I could eat or go and get that drink. And if I remembered right, Riggs' had wings. Damn good ones.

Riggs' was a bar owned by a nice guy. He'd given me a once-over the first time I walked into the place, and I had simply smiled and shaken my head. I wasn't interested in starting anything, especially not with the bartender I wanted to get to know personally when it came to my drinks.

I tugged off my tie and made my way to Riggs', grateful that it didn't seem too busy on a weeknight. Once I got out of the car, I looked down at my slacks, nice shoes, and the button-up shirt I had on and figured I was probably a little overdressed for the place. But I wasn't about to go home and change. I rolled up my sleeves so my forearms were bare and undid the button nearest my neck. It was the closest I could get to casual. Plus, I didn't usually wear jeans. It just wasn't who I was.

I walked in, the sound of music playing and people talking over drinks and food filling my ears. My shoulders immediately relaxed, and I knew I had come to the right place. I needed people around, but I didn't need to talk to them. Wings and a beer and maybe a whiskey, neat. That's all I needed.

But then I looked over into the corner, saw a familiar set of people, and ground my molars together.

Of course, they would be here.

The fucking Montgomerys were everywhere.

CHAPTER 7

Annabelle

"Okay, who is the hottie with that strong jaw?"

I looked over my shoulder, then at my best friend, Brenna, and winced. "That would be my neighbor, Jacob Queen."

Eliza, my other best friend, gasped. "That's *Jacob Queen?*"

I sighed and took a deep gulp of my beer.

"I love that whenever we talk about him, we always use both of his names. And someone always says *that Jacob Queen.* Like a title." Paige sighed happily.

I glared at my little sister. "Shove it, Paige."

She wiggled her fingers at me and leaned into her boyfriend. "Oh, I don't believe I will. And look, Jacob's not headed this way. He did that head-tilt thing, though. Mr. Queen acknowledged your presence, but he isn't coming over here to talk to the big, bad Montgomerys."

"Probably because he knows that while the brothers haven't seen him yet, they will likely kill him because they are big, mean, and love to act like linebackers protecting their quarterback."

I whispered the last part, and both Eliza and Brenna started laughing into their hands, doing their best not to make too much noise.

Jacob sat at the bar, Riggs grinning down at him as the two of them laughed over something. Riggs set a beer and a water in front of Jacob, as well as a menu.

"He shouldn't sit and eat all alone," Eliza said. "It's not nice."

"You shouldn't be so mischievous. You are a lovely, pleasant, *married* woman. Aren't married ladies supposed to be calm and happy and not annoying?" I asked.

"I have no idea where you heard or read that," Eliza said. "And my husband is deployed, so I need some entertainment in my life. If that means joking around about a certain dark-haired, chiseled-jawed stranger at a bar for you? Well, I'm going to have fun."

"Oh, yes, that sounds like a plan." Brenna clapped her hands as she grinned.

"I don't like you guys." I pouted.

"Don't pout. You're an adult," Paige said, her eyes dancing with laughter.

Her boyfriend, Colton, cleared his throat. "If it's all right with you, I'm going to go get grilled by Paige's brothers rather than sit here listening to this. I feel like I don't have enough estrogen, and I'm eavesdropping on the secret meeting of an organization I shouldn't know about."

He grinned, and I rolled my eyes before Paige went up on her tiptoes to kiss him soundly. I averted my gaze because some things having to do with my little sister I did not need to see.

"He seems nice," Brenna said, watching Colton walk away.

My sister smiled. "He's great. He makes me laugh, he's kind, he has a good job, and he isn't riddled with debt."

Eliza laughed. "And that's what you're worried about?" she asked.

Paige shook her head. "No, that's what my dad would worry about, so I'm learning to tack it on for when I'm around him. Sorry. I'm just trying to get used to the idea that I have a committed boyfriend. Not some guy I date for a couple of days and never see again. And it's not like a high school boyfriend where it's all about weird anxiety and wanting to throw up."

I looked at Brenna and analyzed that comment, then we all snorted, holding back our laughter. "I'm sorry, but high school boyfriends make you want to throw up?" I asked, pressing my lips together after I'd said the words.

"You know what I mean. When we were younger, it was always stressful and anxiety-riddled because of social constructs inherent within school walls. This feels nice."

"So, it's serious?" Eliza asked.

"Maybe."

I listened with half an ear as my friends and Paige began discussing Colton and all his qualities. I liked the guy, but I didn't know him well enough to judge. He'd have to run the Montgomery gauntlet if he wanted to go the distance with Paige. And not because we were overprotective. Okay, not *only* because we were overprotective. Mainly because Paige wouldn't date anybody seriously without us loving him. We were family, and that's how we worked.

It had been different with Jonah because it hadn't been real. And Paige hadn't even been old enough to drive, so I knew she didn't have as many memories of him as I did. There hadn't been love there. Not the kind shared between a husband and his wife. But there had been love between two best friends who didn't want to leave each other alone in the dark.

I shook away those melancholic thoughts as Eliza looked at me, her gaze troubled.

"What's wrong?" my best friend asked. She'd pulled her dark hair away from her face tonight, all twisted together on the top of her head. It would tumble around her shoulders later when we danced, and she would look like a beautiful princess in the woods, carefree and happy. I knew she missed her husband with each passing day. And Marshall would be coming home soon, God willing. I didn't know how she did it day in and day out, but she was a force to be reckoned with and a light in all of our lives. It helped that she was brilliant, sweet, and always had my back.

"Okay, seriously, what is with you?" Brenna asked.

Brenna had dark hair, fair skin, and the most kissable lips I had ever seen. At least, that's what one of our guy friends back in college had said when he was drunk and had pulled away from very kissable Brenna. She was gorgeous, and I had never actually seen her go on a date before. She might razz Paige and me about relationships and the men in our lives, but Brenna did not date.

I would love to know why, but I had a feeling I knew exactly why. I looked over her shoulder at the group of my brothers and held back a wince.

That was why.

"I think I need to dance," I said. My brain was going in a thousand different directions, and I couldn't focus.

"Dancing would be good," Eliza said, studying my face. "Or maybe you should go over and see if Jacob Queen needs anything."

"He is my neighbor. He's Jonah's brother," I whispered fiercely. All three sets of eyes softened, and I could have cursed myself. "Okay, no bad feelings. These are happy times. It is our weeknight, single beer, dancing night. We all have to go to work in the morning, so let's make sure we get our dancing out of the way now so we can go to sleep early."

"You're so responsible," Paige said as if she weren't the first person at the office each day.

"Go see Jacob."

"Too late," Brenna said, wincing, and I looked over as Archer, Benjamin, Beckett, and the two boyfriend tagalongs made their way to the bar.

"Oh, God, no. No, no, no, no, no."

Paige snorted. "I cannot believe that Colton and Marc are going along with this."

"I think they probably just didn't want to be left behind," Eliza said. "I mean, it's a lot of testosterone and posturing. Look at them being like peacocks, fluttering around that poor, sweet man at the bar all alone, needing to be rescued..."

I flipped off my best friend, and she laughed, Brenna and Paige joining in.

"I hate you all." I stomped my way over to the bar where my brothers were now glowering down at Jacob, who was calmly licking his thumb, trying to get some wing sauce off.

My gaze zeroed in on his tongue as it swiped over his skin, and I swallowed hard, telling myself that I was losing my mind. It was hot. And I was parched. That's all it was.

I was not having deliciously decadent thoughts about Jacob Queen's tongue. There were things that I shouldn't do. Lines I could not cross. And weird, sweaty thoughts about where that tongue might go on my body was not something I should ever think about.

Of course, now it was the *only* thing I was thinking about.

I hated him, remember? Yes, that helped. I might be saving his life right now, but that was only because I was a good person, not because I liked him. I still hated Jacob Queen.

And if I made that my mantra, I might be able to make it through the day. To their credit, both Archer's and Paige's boyfriends were off to the side, talking to each other, keeping an eye on the group at the bar but not joining in.

I eyed them, and they both held up their hands in mock-innocence before taking a step back as if they'd choreo-graphed it. They looked at each other before they burst out laughing and then walked back over to the girls.

I narrowed my eyes at them as they left and mouthed the word: *cowards*.

Archer's boyfriend shrugged, and they took my seat and one of the empty ones at the girls' table.

Okay, time to do this.

"What are we talking about?" I asked, putting my arms around the twins' waists. Both Beckett and Benjamin glared down at me.

"We're just seeing what Jacob's up to," Archer said, grin-ning as he leaned on the bar on Jacob's opposite side. Oh, Archer might be the one that smiled and was a little more jovial when it came to his needling, but I worried about him the most. Because while my brothers could bodily carry Jacob out of Riggs' and make sure he never yelled at me or called me names again, Archer would be the one to hurt him. My sweet, kind, twin baby brother would make sure that Jacob rued the day he'd even so much as spoke a harsh word to or about me.

"Hi, Annabelle," Jacob said, his eyes full of humor though not fear. Silly man, he didn't understand the precarious position he was in. He wiped his hands on the napkin in front of him and looked me right in the eyes.

"What are we doing over here, boys?" I asked again, focusing on my brothers rather than Jacob. Not because I didn't want to look at him, but because I knew it was necessary to make sure my brothers didn't do anything. Yet I could feel Jacob's gaze on me, and I wondered why. I shouldn't. He had hated me for how many years? He couldn't suddenly want to stare at me the way I thought he was. Maybe he imagined hating me even more. That was it. It was still loathing, something he was trying to hide, though wasn't doing a very good job of.

"We were just seeing how Jacob likes his wings," Beckett said, far too smoothly.

"Okay, Montgomerys," Riggs said as he strolled over to us. "Y'all are not bar fighters. Let's not become them."

"It's not going to be a problem," Benjamin said, his voice cool.

"Of course, not. Jacob's an old friend." Benjamin smiled slowly.

"Seriously, stop it," I said. "This is enough."

"What's enough?" Beckett asked, and I narrowed my eyes at him.

"Please. People are starting to stare."

The man in question cleared his throat. "I'm pretty sure

they always stare when the Montgomerys are together. You guys tend to take up a lot of space."

I rolled my eyes before I glared at Jacob. "You're not helping the situation."

Jacob wiped his hands on his napkin once again before he slowly drained the rest of his beer, his gaze not leaving mine. Was he trying to get beat up by my brothers? Or maybe me? Perhaps I would be the one who swung first.

"Let's dance," Jacob said, startling me.

"Excuse me?" Archer asked, his eyes wide.

"What? I came here for a beer, wings, and maybe a dance. Come on, Annabelle. Help me get to know my old hometown."

"Jacob," I whispered.

"What do you think you're doing?" Benjamin asked, while Beckett moved closer.

I tugged on their belt loops. Thankfully, the twins moved back. "Come on, let's get out of their way before they hurt you," I muttered.

"I am shocked," Beckett said. "I would never hurt a fellow human being."

I resisted the urge to roll my eyes again. I held out my hand, and Jacob slid his palm into mine. He stood, and I ignored the warmth of him and the fact that my brothers were all watching.

"Come on, let's head to the dance floor. Your brothers aren't going to beat me up. They were only crowding me because I was an asshole before. And I deserved it. If they did hit me, I would probably deserve that, too. I mean, I was a jerk to you. They should stand up for you. That's what brothers do."

He met my gaze, and my shoulders slumped. "Why are you being so nice?" I asked as he led me to the dance floor.

"Come on, Annabelle, dance with me." He put a hand around my back, the other holding mine, and I swallowed hard.

"Why are you doing this?" I asked.

"I don't know," he said as if unaware that he was saying the words. "I saw you, and I wanted to dance. It's probably the most idiotic thing I could have done, but here we are."

"Here we are," I repeated.

"So, those are your brothers these days, huh? How are the twins doing?"

"They are just fine. As is Archer. The other two guys, the ones that walked away, are Archer's and Paige's boyfriends."

"Who are the girls with Paige?"

My gaze shot up. "You remember what Paige looks like? After all these years?"

"She looks like you, though a little younger, a little more innocent."

I narrowed my gaze. "Did you just call me a not-so-innocent, aging woman?"

Jacob winced. "I meant to say that I like the looks of you, and it came out weird."

"Oh," I said, not exactly sure what to say to that. "Well, it was weird. You don't need to call me old or experienced."

Jacob winced again. "I'm trying to be nice. Because I want to, not because I said I would. It's coming out as me being a jerk."

"Well..." I said, trailing off.

He snorted. "I see." He sighed. "I am a jerk," he repeated.

"You don't have to keep calling yourself that. You apologized. And now look at us, nearly acting civilized except for the fact that you called me ancient."

"I did not."

"I'm pretty sure you did."

"Anyway, who are the other two girls?"

"My friends, Eliza and Brenna. Brenna is single, but Eliza's married."

Jacob narrowed his eyes. "And why are you telling me that?"

"I don't know, you seemed interested."

"Only in dancing with you, darling Annabelle."

I nearly tripped over his feet, but he kept me steady, the pressure of his hand on the small of my back firm. "What are you doing, Jacob?"

"I have no fucking clue."

The song ended, and he looked at me, swallowed hard, and nodded. "Good night, Annabelle."

I let out a breath. "Bye, Jacob," I whispered.

And then he walked away, leaving me standing on the edge of the dance floor near Brenna, Eliza, and Paige.

"What was that?" Paige asked, coming to my side.

"Oh, just a distraction to get him away from the brothers."

I watched as Jacob nodded at my brothers on the other side of the dance floor before leaving money on the bar for Riggs and heading out. He had danced with me, said odd things, made me feel even more inexplicable things, and then walked away. What the hell was going on?

I cleared my throat. "I'm going to go now."

"Did he say something to you?" Beckett asked.

I huffed out a breath and then grabbed my bag. "No. Jacob danced with me because he wanted to get away from you. That was the only reason." *The only reason it could be.* "He danced and found a way to get out of the place without you guys acting all caveman and beating him up. He took a chance, and now he's gone. I danced, I had wings, nachos, and beer. I'm bloated, and I'm tired. I'm going home."

"Seriously? That's what you're going with?" my twin asked, and I narrowed my eyes at Archer.

"Hey, that's enough of that," I said. "I love you all. I do. Okay, I love most of you. I don't really know you two," I said to the boyfriends as they laughed at me. "But, seriously, I'm an adult. Like all of you. Go out and do whatever you want to do. Go pick up ladies, go dancing, do what you want. I don't care. I'm not your keeper. Just like you're not my keeper. Now, let me be."

"Jacob Queen? Seriously?" Beckett asked.

I closed my eyes and resisted the urge to scream. "He's my...friend. We're trying to be anyway. He's my neighbor, and we still have a lot in common because of his parents. That's not going to change." I saw something shift in Beckett's expression. I didn't know if it was pity or worry—maybe a mixture of both. I didn't care. I didn't have the energy anymore. "Again, I love you all. Now, I'm going home. Have a great night."

"You're welcome to leave, but we're going to grill you later," Brenna said, while Eliza nodded.

I scrunched up my nose at them. "Please, don't. Nothing happened. You all saw, it was only dancing."

"Sexy dancing," Eliza said, and I flipped her off.

"Not very ladylike," Brenna said, so I flipped her off using my other hand.

We all laughed, while Paige clapped her hands behind the girls. "Wow, this is going to be interesting."

"It's not. And I can't deal with all of you right now. Now, darlings, get out of my way."

Thankfully, they did. I made my way out of the bar, got into my car, then drove home, doing my best not to think about Jacob Queen. That, of course, meant that's all I did. I couldn't stop thinking about him. About how it felt with his hand on my back, the way he looked at me. What the hell was going on with that man? Was he trying to be my friend but not doing a very good job of it?

I had to be imagining the heat and whatever the hell attraction was flaring between us. Because thinking about him in that way would be wrong.

Very, very wrong. And yet, I was terrified that maybe it wasn't. Perhaps I wasn't allowing myself to think anything else.

I pulled into my driveway and noticed Jacob's light on. Thankfully, it didn't seem like he noticed me or wanted to come outside. Not that I thought he would. Because, after all, it had only been a distraction.

I needed to stop overthinking.

I got out of the car just as another vehicle pulled into the driveway of the house next to me. Hotch got out and waved as he walked toward his front door. I waved back, wondering why I couldn't like a nice man like him. Why did I have to start having weird feelings about a man I didn't even know. A man I shouldn't want.

I was going inside to take a bath, and then I would go to bed, alone, to get ready for the workday. Because that's what I needed to focus on. Work and family. Not a man I knew I would dream about once again.

The one person I knew I shouldn't.

CHAPTER 8

Jacob

I groaned as I looked over my paperwork and leaned back against my couch to take a sip of coffee. I needed a couple of hours off to get a few household chores done, and work on my yard, things that any new homeowner should focus on.

Yet I knew I wouldn't be able to do any of that until I focused on what was right in front of me. A woman had given up most of her life and time to take care of her dying mother, and once her mother finally passed after a long battle with cancer, the woman's siblings had come out of nowhere and demanded more money from the will. I was defending the woman, who had lost her mother, hadn't had time to grieve, and was dealing with three siblings who were possibly some of the worst people on the planet.

They hadn't even bothered to visit their dying mother

until it looked as if things were going to take a turn for the worst. They had gone for posterity's sake, not because they were losing the woman who had taken care of them. I had seen that much from meeting them.

I would be the shark my client needed, but it was a lot of stress for her. Therefore, I was doing my best to make sure she won. And since I was down two staff members, I was doing more work than usual on top of relocating.

But we would win this, damn it, I just had to learn that things worked a little bit differently up in Fort Collins than they did in Denver. Who knew an hour or so could change so much? I closed my laptop and stacked the files on top of it, telling myself I would only take a little break. I drained the last of my coffee, wincing as it had gone cold at least thirty minutes ago, and stood up to stretch my back.

Today was technically my day off, not something I usually allowed myself, but my staff had pushed me out the doors the night before and told me not to come back until Monday. Considering I had already threatened to do the same to them, I wasn't sure I liked that we were mothering each other. Though maybe that's what we needed.

I put my work away and went to get myself some water since I'd already had two cups of coffee. Considering it was the weekend, I should probably limit my caffeine intake. Maybe. I looked down at my phone and immediately called my parents because I could. I could go over there right now and check on them, and it wouldn't take me over an hour in traffic to get there. There were reasons I'd moved here, and that was only one of them.

"Hey there," my dad said. "Mom's sleeping."

I paused, not liking the tone of his voice. "You okay?" I asked. I didn't ask if Mom was all right. My father would tell me either way. And first, someone needed to take care of Dad.

"It was a long night, but the nurse is here, doing what she can. Your mom is fine now. She's resting, and we had a good morning. It was just a long night."

I held back a curse and swallowed the lump in my throat. "Good. That's good. Well, not about last night, but this morning. Did you get any sleep?"

I swore I could hear the smile in my father's voice as he answered. "You know I didn't. But I'm about to take a nap and possibly do some yardwork later."

That made me smile even as I pushed away the fear. There wasn't anything I could do but be there for them both. "I was about to do the same. And I should probably clean and vacuum or something."

"Don't you have one of those robot vacuums?"

"I do. Best invention ever."

My dad sighed. "Wish we could have one, but I can't have it tangling up in cords."

"You're using the cleaning service I hired?"

"We are. And I'm forever grateful for you providing that. While I still have the dexterity to get on my hands and knees and clean the tile, I'm glad I don't have to."

"You say the word, and I'll start sending that food service there, too. They send meals already cooked, right to your door."

"Maybe. Right now, we're finding our normal, and I don't think your mom or I are ready for that yet."

"Understood. I would offer to cook for you, but we all know that would only hurt somebody in the end." My dad laughed, and it was the most incredible sound in the world because it sounded real, not tired or forced—just my dad.

"I have no idea how you ended up such a poor cook. Your mother and I both do a decent job in the kitchen, and yet you can't boil an egg."

"I only blackened a pot once while boiling an egg."

"And it was a nice pot. Never did get it clean again."

I laughed and talked to my father for a few more minutes, reminiscing about the good times we'd had, something that we needed to do more often. These days, it seemed I only wallowed in the bad parts—Jonah, Susan, and now Mom. There needed to be good parts, too. If not, it would only get harder and harder to make it through each day.

We said our goodbyes, making sure we said, "I love you." It had been something that Jonah had always ensured we did, no matter what. As we left the conversation, we had to tell each other that. Even if we were exhausted or fighting, we had to say it. Because the words were true, and you never knew when they would be your last.

And on that melancholic note, I slid my phone into my jeans' pocket and went to get the tools from my garage. I opened the big door and walked out to my flowerbed and looked down at the project in front of me. Whoever had moved in before me had put in a bunch of mini rose bushes and a fern thing that I didn't know the name of. I had no idea what I was doing with them and would probably end up hiring someone, but I needed to do something with my hands now, and this was it.

I moved to my hands and knees and pulled out some weeds—at least I hoped they were weeds—scowling at the things. How was it that they'd popped up so quickly? The real estate agent had said they had taken care of the house right before I moved in, and when I visited the place a couple of times, the weeds weren't here. I swore they grew overnight.

"Be careful of the plant right next to where you're pulling. That's an actual flower that will bloom for you every year. You also have tulip bulbs that will spawn for you, even though Colorado winters sometimes mean they'll come to life in February or late-June."

I looked over at the sound of Annabelle's voice, my gut tightening. It wasn't because I hated her. No, that had been a lie I'd told myself for far too long. It was because she did something to me—something I shouldn't feel.

She walked over, her feet bare in flip-flops, her toes painted a light pink. She had on torn-up jeans and a layered tee-shirt that made her look like she was young enough to be in college, and not a woman with a full-time job as a business owner.

Or a woman who was also a widow. I needed to stop thinking about her. She was Jonah's, not mine.

"This?" I asked, pointing my tool at the flower thing.

"It'll be beautiful. And there's no maintenance other than making sure you don't stab it as you're taking care of the weeds." Annabelle went to her knees beside me, her thigh brushing mine. I swallowed hard, annoyed with myself. "Here, come on, let me help."

"You don't have to. Just tell me what to do."

"I just pulled out my weeds. Now, I'm going to tell you how to do yours without massacring the whole thing."

She gently shoved me out of the way, and I fell to my side, laughing.

"You're violent," I accused.

"Perhaps. But you deserved it. Okay, now do you have trimmers?"

"Like for a tree?"

She rolled her eyes, her smile wide. "No, for a bush. The little ones that snap together so you can trim?"

I shook my head. "No, I didn't have those at my other place."

"Okay, I have some. We'll get it done."

"You don't have to help me, Annabelle. I can buy trimmers."

"You can, and you will. But first, I'm going to teach you how to help your garden, although I am surprised you haven't hired someone."

I shrugged. "I don't know who to hire."

"Benjamin doesn't do many smaller jobs anymore, but he can always add you to his rotation if you want. Or I can put you in touch with someone else."

I frowned. "Your brother?"

She nodded. "He's a landscape architect. He's brilliant and works on projects for small homes, neighborhoods, and also giant gardens that are part of the Montgomery purview, but not necessarily projects that all of the other family members work on."

"How is it working with your siblings? It has to be a lot."

"It's interesting. Most of us get along all the time, and we have a new member of the team that works in the building with us. Clay. He is sort of like a son to one of my cousins."

"That sounds like a story."

"A very long one that's not mine to tell. But my cousin, Storm, down in Denver, has been friends with Clay for a while. When Clay graduated college and was looking for a job, Storm and Beckett talked, and then Clay moved up here with his three cousins."

"I guess it pays to know a Montgomery."

"We will rule the world one day. Although I think it's just in terms of numbers," she said on a laugh. "Okay, now let me get those clippers, and I'll show you what you need to do." She stood up and wiped her palms on her pants. I tried not to notice how her jeans encased her ass, but damn it, it was right there. I could reach out and touch her. Though I wouldn't because that would be wrong.

What was wrong with me?

She walked into her garage, and I swallowed hard and focused on dealing with my mulch, pressing it down and moving it around even though I had no idea what I was doing yet.

"Hey there," a man said from behind me. I started and turned around.

He had a kind smile, bright eyes, and stood with his hands on his hips.

"You must be the new neighbor. I'm Hotch."

He held out his hand, and I looked up at it, awkwardly standing to shake it. "Jacob."

"Welcome to the neighborhood. I'm on the other side of Annabelle. Glad we're sandwiching her, you know? A woman living alone and all that. Nice to make sure she's safe."

My brows rose. "I guess so. Though I'm pretty sure she can take care of herself."

Hotch laughed. "Oh, she can. And one day, she will go out with me."

"Hotch," Annabelle said, rolling her eyes. "Stop pestering Jacob."

"I was just trying to pester you since I saw you coming. Anyway, I'm headed over to work with Builders for Humanity. We're building some homes on the other side of 25."

I nodded, remembering the sign for the project site when I'd moved here. "I saw that when I drove up. It looks like a worthwhile effort."

"Should be. I thought you were working on it today," Hotch mentioned, and Annabelle shook her head.

"No, we were on it last weekend. I'll be working on it in another two weeks, I think." She looked over at me. "My family and I regularly donate where we can, and we alternate who can work on the main project. It's my day off today, so I'm trying to catch up on my household chores, but I think Clay is down there, representing the family."

She smiled as she said it, and I found it nice that she considered someone who worked with her family like I did with my staff.

"Well, we're going to miss you. Have a great day. Nice to meet you, Jacob."

Hotch waved and then headed back to his house, taking the sidewalk so as not to walk on our lawns.

"Nice guy," I said, frowning.

"You said that, yet you're practically scowling. Hotch's a good guy. He's just friendly."

"Why did you snarl when you said *friendly?*"

"I have no idea. I'm friendly. I like people. But Hotch has like…an emphasis on friendly. I once thought about setting him and Paige up because I felt like their energies would match, but then she met Colton, and I figured if it didn't work out, I didn't want my neighbor and my sister to have dated."

"Yeah, that would probably be a bad idea. Plus, I'm pretty sure he has the hots for you, and that would be awkward."

"I'm not dating him either. You think having a sister

dating your neighbor's bad? I am never going to date my neighbor." She winced and then beamed at me. "Sorry."

"Ouch," I said. I wondered why that dig hurt. I didn't want her to date me. Maybe I needed to start adding Bailey's Irish cream to my coffee in the morning on the weekends. I was losing my damn mind.

"Okay, let's get to work."

"You do not have to help me."

"I'm in the mood, and I'm being nice. It's a neighborly thing. You can make me lunch."

I laughed. "I was just telling my dad that I can't cook. I can probably make you a pasta salad from a box. Will that work?"

"That sounds lovely. I love pasta. Even though I probably shouldn't have it."

My gaze traveled down her curves, and I cleared my throat and then met her eyes. Her pupils dilated, and she licked her lips.

Hell, she'd caught me looking. And it seemed she liked it.

Again, what was wrong with me?

"You can eat as much pasta as you want," I muttered and shook my head. "Anyway, let's get to gardening."

"And you can tell me how your parents are doing, I was going to call them earlier, but I hate bugging them."

We both went down to our hands and knees again and worked on the garden. I shook my head. "I don't think you could ever be a bother to them, Annabelle."

She froze for a second before tilting her head at me. "That is a sudden change of heart," she said carefully.

"I'm trying, Annabelle. Not doing a perfect job of it, but I'm trying."

She smiled, swallowed hard, and we both went back to work.

By the time we were done gardening, we were covered in dirt, laughing, and we had done her backyard, mine, and my front yard—she had already worked on her front yard by the time I came outside. And now I knew way too much about gardening.

I hated it.

"I'm going to call your brother. I know he probably won't work on my yard because he hates me, but he has to know somebody I can use."

Annabelle laughed as she washed her hands in the sink while I started the water to boil for the pasta.

"He doesn't hate you." She paused. "Okay, he might a little, but he'll like you when he gets to know who you are now. I did, eventually."

"Okay, that hurt."

"Sorry, we're just very good at that."

"It seems we are. Now, I have soda, water, and lemonade that I made to make my mom happy, but I don't really drink it."

"If it's still good, I'll drink it," Annabelle said, shaking her head. "And you know I was kidding about lunch. But now I'm starving, so thank you."

"I put you to work doing manual labor. I think the least I can do is feed you some semi-crunchy pasta."

"Maybe I should be making lunch," she said on a laugh.

"No, I can do this. I hope."

She laughed again and then moved out of the way so I could get her some lemonade. We made the pasta, and I cooled it down quickly while she stirred up the olive oil, water, and the seasoning packet. We mixed it all together, added cut-up chicken I had from some leftover takeout, and ended up with a decent lunch.

"Hey, this is good," she said. "Probably horrible for you and full of preservatives, but it's been a while since I had one."

"Sometimes it just hits the spot when you don't want to make food or grab a hamburger on your way home."

"Yes. I'm trying to do better about that, so I have lots of salad fixings at home all the time. But maybe I need to start keeping pasta salad fixings. I'm sure I could replicate that with my own seasonings."

"And now I think I'm even hungrier," I said and practically devoured my half of the pasta.

She ate her half, and we cleaned up, laughed, talked, and had a good evening.

"Here, let me help you with the dishes," she said, moving past me. Her skin brushed mine. I still had a hard time telling myself that it was only me. I saw the heat in her gaze, the way she bit her lip, and I wondered what was going on.

The tension in the kitchen was palpable, yet I told myself I imagined it. But as my hand brushed against hers under the water, she didn't move back. Instead, the sharp intake of her breath set me on edge.

We put away the dishes, chatting, but I didn't think either of us knew what we talked about. And then she turned to me, her mouth parted, and her eyes wide. "I think... I think maybe... I don't know."

I leaned forward, both of us moving closer to the counter. "I don't know either." I reached out, telling myself this was wrong, but I couldn't hold back. I brushed my knuckle down her cheek, and she gasped, leaning in to my touch.

"What are you doing?" she asked.

"I don't know. But I'm going to kiss you now." And then I met her gaze again before I lowered my mouth to hers. She tasted of lemonade and pasta, and something new that had to be all Annabelle.

I let out a sigh, and she gently put her hands on my hips, parting her lips for me. I deepened the kiss, aching for more, not able to hold back. Her hand slid up my back, and I cupped her face, needing, tasting.

"Tell me to stop." I groaned, then leaned my forehead against hers, trying to catch my breath.

She tugged on my shirt. "Don't stop."

So, I didn't. I kissed her again, and then I wrapped my arms around her, put my hands on her ass, and lifted her. She let out a gasp, and then I captured her mouth with mine, needing her more. I rested her butt on the edge of the counter, pressing into her, my cock hard behind my zipper.

"Jacob," she muttered.

I kissed her again, needing her, my hands now in her hair. She tugged on my shirt, and I moved back to pull it over my head.

Her gaze moved to my chest, and she let out a slow breath before raking her nails down my flesh. I hummed, tugging at her shirts, and she helped me pull them over her head. And then my hands were over her bra, cupping her.

"You're so fucking beautiful," I muttered.

"Look who's talking," she whispered.

Her breasts were full, her nipples tight against the fabric. She overfilled the cups, her chest rising and lowering rapidly as she fought for breath, as both of us fought for control.

She reached around, her gaze on mine, and undid the clasp of her bra. The lingerie fell, her breasts bouncing ever so slightly, and I reached out to brush my knuckle across her rosy nipple.

"Beautiful," I mumbled and then leaned forward to capture one with my lips. She moaned, sliding her hand through my hair, and I suckled her. Then I moved to her other breast, molding her, paying as much attention to her body as I could.

"I love your tits," I said on a harsh chuckle, and she laughed, as well.

"I love you loving them," she said, her voice deeper. She had one leg wrapped around my waist, the other spread and hooked over my hip. I slid my hands down her body and tugged on the button of her jeans. Her gaze moved to mine, and she nodded. I undid her pants, grateful that she helped me by lifting her butt so I could wiggle them down her legs. They fell to the floor, and she sat there in little pink panties that barely covered her. I groaned again, then dropped to my knees, grateful that my counters were at the perfect height. And then I looked at her beautiful covered pussy and blew cool air over her.

"I'm going to fucking taste you."

"Then do it," she said, sounding like the Annabelle I was getting to know, the one who knew what she wanted, and I was grateful for it.

I pushed all thoughts of how this could be wrong and how we were probably fucking this up out of my head. I didn't have time for that. Not when I craved the deliciousness before me. I slid her panties to the side, gazed at the glistening flesh in front of me, and then latched myself to her pussy.

Her hips shot off the counter, and she wrapped her legs around my neck. I moaned, flicking at her clit as I licked and sucked. Then I speared her with two fingers. She came, her mouth open on a silent scream, her full lips looking delectable.

I gazed up at her, and she peered down at me, her eyes dark. I swallowed hard. I kept kissing her, licking, and then I stood up and leaned forward to meet her mouth. I crushed my lips to hers, tangling my fingers in her hair. She arched into me, her pussy wet against my jeans. And then she was suddenly undoing the snap on my pants, unzipping me. She slid her hand behind the elastic of my boxer briefs and gripped me.

I let out a breath, sucking air through my teeth to try not to come right then.

She pumped me slowly, and I cursed, hating myself for not being able to focus. I blindly reached out for my wallet on the counter, dug for a condom, and pulled away slightly. I kissed her again, needing to taste her, to fall into oblivion so I wouldn't think too hard.

I ripped open the condom packet, slid the latex over my dick, and didn't even bother to pull my pants off completely. I positioned myself at her entrance and met her gaze. At her nod, I slammed home.

We both gasped out a breath, her pussy tight like a vise around me. I shook, needing control. And then she met my gaze, leaned forward, and bit my lip. I grinned, gripped her hips in a bruising hold, and moved.

I fucked her on the counter, both of us panting, egging each other on as I moved more frantically, slamming home over and over again. And when she came again, my thumb over her clit, all that remained was desire and need and temptation. No worry or anxiety.

I came with her, needing her. Not thinking about the fact

that I could have just fucked everything up. All I could think about was Annabelle touching me, the way it felt, her taste, how she came around my cock. And the fact that I didn't want this to be over.

And even if it meant me going to hell, I wanted to do it again.

CHAPTER 9

Annabelle

y legs were still wrapped around Jacob's waist as I leaned back and let out a breath. My lips were swollen, my hair tousled, my breasts heavy and covered in tiny little bite marks from the person currently still deep inside me. Jacob leaned down, his whole body shaking as he swallowed hard. Neither of us spoke until he cleared his throat.

"I think...I think I should clean us up."

I looked up at him and nodded, not sure what to say. The brother of the boy I had married for friendship rather than love, and the man who had hated me up until last week, was currently balls-deep inside me, after coming hard—after I had come even harder around him. Not once, not twice, but *three* times.

"Yes, I think we should clean up."

He pulled out of me, and I winced at the ache, knowing I would be sore later. "Shit, are you okay?"

Well, that was a loaded question. Okay? Not even a little. But I didn't think that was what he was asking. At least, not yet.

"I'm fine. Really. It's just been a while. And you're uh, well, not small."

His lips quirked into a smile, and I resisted the urge to roll my eyes at the male pride I saw in his expression.

Yes, he had a big dick. And, apparently, he knew how to use it. And his mouth. And his hands. And now my breasts were heavy again, and I wanted to press my thighs together to relieve the ache.

Damn him.

Damn all of this.

"I'll be right back," he said as he tucked himself back into his jeans and presumably went off to get a towel or something. I wasn't a hundred percent sure why since he had perfectly good kitchen towels right there, but I had never had kitchen sex before. Maybe one had to clean themselves off in the bathroom and not in the kitchen. Perhaps I should simply run away and forget this ever happened.

But as I tried to slide my way off the counter, considering I wasn't wearing anything but the panties he had shoved to the side, I wasn't sure if I would be able to leave at all. Because I didn't know where he had tossed my bra after we'd moved our pile of clothes. And I needed that.

Plus, I knew if I ran away, we'd still have to talk about this. Or say it was fun and never happen again, or shout and yell at each other. Something. Maybe the latter would be the best option. We'd get everything out of our systems and wouldn't have to talk about it again.

I searched around the kitchen until I found my bra hanging over the bar chair and winced as I reached over to put it on.

"Wait a minute," Jacob said before bringing a towel towards me. He moved slowly as if afraid I'd bolt, and I didn't blame him. He pushed my hair off my shoulder and brushed my lips with his thumb. "Hey," he said.

"Hey," I whispered.

And then he slid the warm towel between my legs, and I groaned, my hands digging into his arms, not having even realized I had moved up to hold him.

"I know you're sore. I just wanted to take care of you."

I closed my eyes, letting out a breath as he painstakingly took care of me and then helped me dress.

It was the sweetest and most erotic thing that anyone had ever done for me.

And we were still standing in his kitchen.

Afterward, when we were both dressed, he handed me a glass of water, neither of us speaking as we drank.

"So," he began.

"So," I repeated.

"I didn't mean for that to happen," he said, and I flinched. I hadn't meant to, but I hated that phrase. It sounded as if he already regretted it. I hadn't even had time to process what had just happened, at least not enough to regret it.

He shook his head quickly, reached out, and brushed his thumb along my lips again.

I wanted to lick that digit, suck it into my mouth, but I didn't.

There was no time for that. And it wouldn't help me think.

"I was saying I didn't expect that, hadn't planned on it. Because I never let myself think about you in that way."

My eyes widened. "*Let* yourself?"

"You were younger than me when we knew each other before. Young enough that it would have been improper as hell for me to want you beyond thinking you were cute."

"Oh."

He smiled, and it did wonderful and far too alluring things to his eyes. "Yeah, oh. And then you were hanging out with my brother, and I figured you two were together."

"Never, um...not in the way you think." I quickly shook my head.

"He would've told me if you had," he said, and I blushed.

"Yes, he probably would have."

"And then later, we were going in two separate directions, and I hated you as much as I hated myself."

My head shot up. "What?"

"I told myself I hated you so I wouldn't have to think about what I was missing, *who* I was missing. I was wrong, and I'm going to spend a hell of a lot of time trying to make it up to you."

I quickly shook my head. "You don't need to make up for anything. You've already done enough."

His gaze went to the counter where we'd just had sex, and I blushed even harder.

"That's not what I meant."

"I know, but I like the way you blush."

I groaned and licked my lips. "Jacob, like you said, I didn't expect that either."

"You're right. Neither of us did. And I don't know what's going to happen next, but I'm glad it happened."

My eyes widened. "You're glad?"

He shrugged, then drained his glass of water before putting it in the sink. "I don't know. I feel like we've been dancing around each other for the past couple of weeks. Or maybe I'm losing my mind."

I bit my lip. "Well, we did dance."

He smirked. "Yeah, we did."

"I just...I'm not sure us being in a relationship is smart. Especially with everything that has happened between us in the past and what might happen in the future with your family."

His eyes clouded over, and I hated that I'd brought it up. But he had moved here for his mother, and I was still part of their lives because I loved them.

We were both slowly watching a woman we loved fade away. It was devastating, achingly painful, and there was no fixing it.

"You're right. There is an attraction, though."

"Yes. I mean, I wouldn't have done that with you if I wasn't attracted."

He smiled, making him look even more handsome, and I kind of hated him for it. "I'm not looking for anything serious, Annabelle," he said, his voice low. "And I know we probably should have talked about that before we did what we just did. We probably should have talked about a lot of things. But I didn't only come here for my mother."

I frowned. "I thought that's why you moved back to Fort Collins."

He nodded. "That was part of it. But I needed a fresh start. My divorce has only been final for a few months."

I blinked and nearly staggered back at the nonexistent blow. I didn't know why it felt like one in the first place. "You were married?" I asked. "Your parents never mentioned it."

He grimaced. "I don't think they liked Susan."

"So they just ignored the fact you were married? That doesn't sound like the couple I know."

He sighed. "They were always nice to her, and there's even a picture of our wedding in their bedroom in that little nook area."

"I haven't ever been in there," I added.

"It's Mom's sanctuary, so there are family photos in there." He paused. "There's a photo of your wedding, too."

I winced, my heart aching. "I have one in my home also."

"There's a photo of you around here somewhere. Mom and Dad gave it to me, and I didn't have the heart to throw it away. It was Jonah, you know?" He looked around as I thought on that more. "I haven't finished unpacking. Don't have everything on the walls yet. As I said, I'm starting over. Susan and I didn't work out. For a lot of reasons. And my parents were right. We didn't fit, but I tried. Maybe a little too hard. But I'm finally figuring out what I want, and a serious relationship isn't it."

I shrugged and looked down at my hands. "Same for me."

His gaze shot to mine as I looked up. "Really?"

"Really. Not every woman wants marriage and babies and a white picket fence. I can build my own fence if I want to. I can design the best house to live in. Alone. In fact, I already did. I got married too young, and now every time I imagine a wedding or marriage or something like that when I'm part of it, I think of Jonah."

He flinched. "Damn."

"Yes. Damn. It's silly, and it shouldn't happen, but I don't know... I don't know if I ever want anything serious. I love my job, and I'm good at it, and I'm focusing most of my attention on that right now. And my family." I paused. "And

I'll be honest, I'm not very good at the whole relationship thing anyway."

"Well, as evidenced by my divorce, neither am I," he said dryly. He looked at me then, and I didn't know what else to say. "So, are we saying that we're going to walk away from this and continue being neighbors who try to be friends? Or what?"

"Or what maybe," I paused. "I don't know what I want, Jacob. But I had fun," I teased.

His eyes lightened. Thankfully. "So did I." A pause. "Maybe we can try this thing out. You and me. Nothing serious, only friends, finding fun. And perhaps a little peace."

My heart lightened at that because I *did* have fun. And I hadn't been lying to him. I didn't want anything serious. But the idea of maybe having someone to talk to, someone to be with where it wasn't just me alone in my bedroom all the time sounded nice.

"Would we ever go out on a date?" I asked, not knowing why I needed to broach the subject.

He frowned, and I winced.

"Okay, no dating."

He shook his head. "No, but I don't know the rules for this. I dated a lot in high school and college, but then I found Susan, and we got married. I haven't dated as an adult with a job and a house. I don't know how it works."

That made me laugh. "I don't know either. I'm pretty much a hermit. The only times I ever go out are with my family and the girls when they get time off. And you've seen my brothers, they scare away any potential suitors."

"They didn't scare me away."

I swallowed hard. "No, I think we scared ourselves enough for that."

That made him laugh. "You're right. As for dating? I could see us going out to eat, doing something like that. Maybe going to the bar and annoying your brothers."

I snorted. "Oh, please, you could not handle all of the Montgomerys."

That made him scowl. "I'm sure I can."

"Famous last words. However, maybe one night. Who knows? We'll just keep it breezy." I laughed. "Or something less clichéd."

"That we can do."

He stepped forward, slid his thumb over my lips again, and then leaned down to capture my mouth. I moaned, my hands going to his waist, fingers slipping through his belt loops.

"I should go," he whispered. "Even though it's my house, I need to go take a cold shower or something. If I don't, I'm not going to get any more work done today."

I stepped away on shaky legs and grinned. "Then I'm going to leave to get *my* work done. Maybe I'll see you around."

"Maybe I'll see you," he said. I turned and left, wondering what the hell I was doing. I was not good at this, but I didn't know if I was terrible at it yet either. It was new, something I'd never done before.

I pulled out my phone as I walked to my house, taking my tools with me.

Me: *Girls, I need help—orange alert.*

A red alert would mean that I needed them over. Orange alert meant that I needed to talk to them.

Eliza: *Are you okay? What happened?*

Brenna: *Does it have to do with that hottie from the bar?*

That made me laugh as I walked into the house, putting everything away.

Me: *I had sex with Jacob Queen in his kitchen, and now we've decided to do a friends-with-benefits thing.*

Eliza: *!!!.*

Brenna: *How was it?*

Brenna: *Was it big?*

Brenna: *I'm coming over.*

I laughed, sank down into my couch, and looked at my phone.

Me: *I have work to do, and so do you. And Eliza is waiting on a call from her hubby. We'll meet up tomorrow as planned.*

Eliza: *You're right, but I will have questions. I'll even make a checklist about it. But are you okay?*

I thought about that and bit my lip.

Me: *I think so. It just sort of happened.*

Brenna: *I hear that's the best way.*

I grinned, shaking my head. Eliza was married, the one who still had a little bit of her wild side but had smoothed out the edges when she got with her husband. She was now the calming one on the texts. I knew Brenna had never been in a serious relationship and was a lot of brashness, all wrapped around a soft, gooey center of innocence.

I loved my best friends, and I was relieved that I hadn't included Paige in this text chain. Mostly because that was my baby sister, and there were things I did not tell her.

Me: *We'll talk tomorrow. But oh my God, I slept with Jacob.*

Brenna: *I see you didn't use his last name.*

Eliza: *It's because he's not just the idea of a man anymore. He's the real deal.*

I groaned.

Me: *He's just a deal. Not the real one. Do your things. I'm going to work.*

Eliza: *Don't work too hard. And be safe.*

Brenna: *And make sure you write down every single detail of exactly how it was so you can tell us and not forget a thing.*

I laughed, texted my goodbyes, and set my phone down. I hadn't meant to sleep with Jacob, though there hadn't been any sleeping going on.

I'd never had sex on a counter before. Never had sex without even a date prior. And I'd certainly never had sex with Jacob.

And now we were going to pretend that everything was normal and maybe do it again.

Somehow, I needed to make like everything was fine. Like I wasn't emotionally churning inside. And I promised myself that I wasn't going to screw it up.

I had a feeling that this promise might be one I would end up breaking.

CHAPTER 10

Jacob

"$\mathcal{D}$ ustin, where is Seressia again?" I asked, rubbing my temples.

"Root canal," Dustin said, wincing.

I looked up at him and grimaced. "Damn. Is she okay?" I inquired, sympathy pouring through me.

"She's doing fine, I guess. She texted that she was going to murder someone, but I didn't know if it was because she had to wait because someone wasn't competent, or because she was in pain. Probably a mixture of both."

"We're running on fumes here," I said, looking at the piles of papers on my desk as well as the emails adding up, one by one, the dings insistent. I didn't usually have notifications on, but I was becoming so tunnel-focused on my case, I kept missing important emails. My staff was wonderful, but we were really shorthanded right now, and I knew if I had been able to stay down south for a bit longer, it might not be this bad. But I'd had to come up north when I did and had to bring my crew with me. We were making do, but today was one of those days.

"We've got it handled," Dustin said. "Well, at least I think we do." The phone rang behind him, and he winced again. "I'll go take care of that."

I laughed. I couldn't help it. "Please. But we've got this. It's almost the end of the day."

"Thank God," the other man said, shaking his head, a smile playing on his lips.

I went back to my paperwork and undid my tie. I'd had court all morning, and thankfully we had won that particular case. But I had court all next week, too, and a deposition. I had assumed many of the clients from Richard, a lawyer I knew from school when he came in for guest visits and then finally retired. I had bought into his practice but kept it as mine, even though it felt like I was starting from the ground up in the end.

Richard had all the faith in the world in me. But right now, I didn't feel like I did.

We were just about at capacity already, and until I got my staff back, we'd be running on those fumes as I had mentioned before. I wasn't in the mood to take on a partner, but having someone to split the work with might help. At least that's what I told myself.

"Call on line four," Dustin called out, and I laughed. He could have sent it straight back with a message, but we were all a little off today, so I didn't mind.

I picked up the phone and had to push all thoughts of stress and other niggling thoughts out of my mind.

"Jacob Queen," I answered.

"Jacob, you want to head down to Denver tonight? The girls and I are going out. New promotion in the office. They'd love to see you."

I looked down at the phone and then glared up at the doorway. Dustin's eyes were wide, his hands moving back and forth.

"*Sorry, wrong call,*" he mouthed, then scurried back to his desk.

Dustin was usually far better at his job. But with Seressia out of the office, and his mother recovering from heart surgery, he was off. We all were. I had offered to let him take the day off and be with his mom, but she was sleeping now. He had spent the morning with her and was taking the next few days off to help out around the house. For now, she was resting, and everything seemed okay. Still, today was a shitty day, and I was ready to close the doors and let everybody go home so we could sage the office or something.

"Jacob? Are you still there?"

I scowled down at the phone, then sucked in a breath through my teeth. "Hey, Susan. Sorry, we're a little busy. No, I can't go down to Denver tonight. I have plans."

"Plans?" she asked, a little anger in her tone.

I wanted to smack myself upside the head for even mentioning it. I should have just said I didn't want to go out. But no, instead, I had intrigued her. I had loved Susan once. But, damn it, I hadn't been the man I needed to be before. That man had tried to love her, had thought he had, but he'd been wrong.

The man I was now didn't even like her.

"I'm busy," I said curtly. "And, Susan, we're divorced. We didn't even *like* each other in the end. What are you doing? What do you hope to accomplish with this?"

She was silent for a moment, and I almost felt bad. But she had used her silences as weapons in the past, though I was trying not to think too hard on that.

"I don't know why you have to be so cruel."

"Susan. Go out with Bob. With your girls. Celebrate the promotion. I'm not the person to celebrate with. Not anymore. We both signed those papers."

"I just miss you, Jacob."

I didn't know if that was true. Wasn't sure if she missed me, or if she missed being the center of someone's world. The problem was, I wasn't sure she had been the center of mine. And that was on me.

"I got to go, my phone's lighting up, and these cases aren't going to deal with themselves."

"Work as usual."

"Goodbye, Susan," I said, sighing. I hung up the phone, not wanting her to suck me back into a conversation I wasn't in the mood to have.

Dustin ran in. "I'm so sorry. I pushed back the wrong line. I just downed a Red Bull, and I'm ready to go. I am so sorry."

I shook my head. "You have a thousand things on your mind. You've never made a mistake like that before, you're not going to again. It's not your fault." I paused. "Okay, it's a little bit your fault, but I don't care right now. Get your work done. I'll do mine, and then we'll head out this Friday night, because what the hell?"

Dustin laughed and went back to his desk.

I stared at my work a bit longer, pushed thoughts of Susan out of my mind, as well as my non-date tonight with a woman I didn't and couldn't hate anymore. What the hell was I thinking? I needed to focus on the job and the people who needed me.

I'd worry about whatever the hell was going on in my life later.

By the end of the evening, I was exhausted, a tension headache coming on hard, but Seressia's root canal had gone well, Dustin's mother was awake, alert, and on the way to a full recovery, and we were taking the weekend off.

Well, as *off* as I normally did.

"I'll see you all on Monday," I ordered. "Take some time for yourselves. If we work ourselves to the bone now, we'll be no use to our clients later when we get swamped."

They all groaned at my attempt at a joke, and we went our separate ways. I needed to go home and change, but first, I wanted to head to my parents'. I'd promised I would stop by to say hello, and that was one thing I wouldn't change, no matter what.

I pulled into the driveway and let myself into the house, not bothering to knock. "Hey, Dad," I said as my father looked up from his recliner. Dad smiled and pulled his glasses away from his face. "Hey, your mom was in her little nook reading. I'm trying to do the same."

"Decided to do it in a different room?" I asked, teasing.

"This is our thirty minutes away from each other so we don't get tired of one another. But I usually only last ten," my father added, grinning.

I saw the sadness in his eyes. Knew why it was there. But I ignored it. There was no use harping when it was evident. We made our way into the bedroom where Mom's reading nook was, and I noticed the photo of Jonah and Annabelle beside her on the table. It was right next to a picture of Susan and me, though both frames were slightly behind a larger one of Jonah and me.

My mother wanted to have the memories close, but I was glad they weren't in my face every time I came over.

"Hey, there's my baby boy," Mom said, holding out her hand towards me. Her fingers were closed, her limb shaking, but she could at least move her arm today slightly. I moved forward and took her hand, kissed her cool skin, and then leaned forward to kiss her cheek.

"Hello, my favorite mom."

"I love being favorites," Mom teased.

"Have a hard day at work, son?" Dad asked as he handed me a glass of water and then put Mom's water bottle next to her, the straw close to her lips.

"It was a tough day. Seressia had a root canal. And Dustin's mother had heart surgery."

"Oh, that's horrible. Is everyone okay?" Mom asked.

"Everybody is on the mend," I answered. "But it was a tough day, and things just piled up. I'm glad we have a weekend to at least be out of the office. I have a few files to go over as usual, but I'm going to try not to work too hard."

"You need to have a life. Go out. Meet someone," my mother said, and I held back a wince, even though it gave me the opening I was looking for. While Annabelle and I planned to be casual and not get too serious, I wasn't going to hide anything. And I knew Annabelle felt the same. I only hoped we didn't screw everything up by doing what we were.

"Well, speaking of getting a life, I'm going out tonight."

Mom's eyes brightened, and my dad grinned. "Really? On a date?" Dad asked, sounding almost incredulous.

I scowled. "I date. You don't need to sound so surprised."

My mom's gaze moved to the photo of Susan, and I

sighed. "Well, I'm at least going to start dating. It's nothing serious, though," I added quickly.

"That's not quite what I like to hear from my son," Mom said.

"We're just taking it slow," I said, thinking that had to be the truth. Though we'd already had sex in my kitchen, so I didn't know if that counted as slow. But it needed to be something. "Actually, I'm taking Annabelle out tonight."

Mom grinned, while dad's eyes narrowed. "Really? Oh, that's wonderful."

"Really? You sure that's wise, son?"

They were reacting as I'd expected them to. But Annabelle and I didn't want secrets, so this is what we were doing.

"We're just taking it slow, hanging out as friends. It might be a date, but it's not too serious. Stop stressing. Both of you. Even if your reasons are opposite each other."

My parents met gazes, a thousand unsaid words sliding between them.

What would it be like to know somebody so well that you didn't have to speak to have an entire conversation? I envied that, even if I knew it would never be for me. I'd tried it with Susan, and it hadn't worked. Now, my dad would, one day soon, not have that anymore. Why would you risk everything for the kind of pain you knew was coming? For the type of pain they'd already felt for Jonah. No, that wasn't for me. I knew I was blessed to at least have a fragment of it with my parents in my life.

"Don't hurt her," my father said, scowling. "It should be serious. It's the two of you. It can get complicated."

I nodded. "We know. That's why we laid out ground rules."

My mom scoffed. "You know, you young children always say you put down ground rules, then you trample all over them. However, I trust you both to make the right decisions and not be stupid little idiots. I am excited, but I won't get too giddy. I think this could be amazing, though."

I shook my head. "You do? And not because you want to see us happy. But is it okay? You know, because of Jonah," I said, voicing what I'd done my best not to think about.

Was I stealing my brother's girl? Was I crossing a line and breaking the code that brothers never dared to speak of? The problem was, Jonah never loved Annabelle the way a husband loves his wife. And I knew that Annabelle felt the same. I didn't know what lines were left to cross. I just hoped I wouldn't be the one breaking the rules.

"I think your brother would want you to be happy. And you haven't been happy, my baby boy," my mother said softly. "You need to be happy. So does Annabelle. And, even if I don't condone this not-serious talk, if you could have even a slight breath of happiness right now, that would be good."

"Good," I said, relief pouring off me. "I promise I won't hurt her. We're not going to be serious enough for us to hurt each other."

My parents once again gave each other a look, but I ignored it.

"And now I need to go home and shower before I pick her up for dinner." I looked down at my watch. "I might be late."

"Hurry, go. Thank you for stopping by. We'll see you on Sunday?" she asked.

"You may see me both days. I love you guys." I swallowed a ball of emotion, kissed both my parents on the cheeks, and then headed out.

My fingers tapped the steering wheel as I thought about

what my parents had said, but I knew that even if I were making a mistake by being with Annabelle, I wasn't wrong in what our plan should be.

It didn't make sense for us to want something more than what we already had.

We could have fun. We could care for one another. And we could remain friends.

That's what needed to happen.

I pulled into my garage and practically leaped out of my car, taking the quickest shower of my life. I pulled on gray slacks and a black, button-up shirt that I figured made me look decent enough for dinner. We were going out for a nice meal, and then planned to come home.

We might do something else, but I wouldn't pressure her, and I knew Annabelle would never pressure me.

I brushed my hair back and noticed that I needed to shave, but it wasn't going to happen in the time I had. I rolled my sleeves up to my elbows and called it good. We weren't going out to a fancy place, and I had noticed Annabelle looking at my forearms before. I might as well let her have a little arm porn tonight. I slid my feet into my shoes, grabbed my wallet, keys, and a couple of condoms, and then headed to my front door.

I opened it, and Annabelle was standing there wearing a pretty, soft-looking, pale pink dress that fit her curves and flared out at mid-thigh. She had on tall heels, carried a little bag, and her dark brown hair floated in the slight breeze. She had done her makeup in a light smoky eye thing, and her lips were glossy and luscious.

I wanted to pull her inside, bend her over the couch, and fuck her hard. I could pull up that little dress, tug her panties to the side again, and slide right home.

My dick pressed against the fly of my pants, and I swallowed hard. "Hey. I was on my way to pick you up."

She grinned. "Well, the good and creepy thing about being neighbors is that I saw you pull in and figured you'd had enough time to shower. I know you're driving. So, here I am. You don't even have to pick me up at my door. See? Super easy."

She was nervous, but hell, so was I. I reached out and pressed my thumb to her chin so I wouldn't mess up her gloss. She parted her lips, letting out a soft breath.

"Hi," I whispered.

"Hi," she breathed.

Damn it. My parents were right. I was going to fuck this up. I would have to figure out a way not to. Right now, I was a goner. There was no way I could keep from being serious. Not unless I tried really hard. But, I reminded myself, I was good at doing what I needed to if I put my mind to it.

So, that was what I would do. I would make sure I didn't do anything too serious. I wouldn't break that rule or cross that line.

Though the Annabelle in front of me was pure temptation, it would have to be one I didn't fall into.

CHAPTER 11

Annabelle

hile marriage and a future beyond my work and family had never been on the table for me, I had never gone into a relationship, as it was, fully cognizant that I didn't want anything more than what I had. I also hadn't gone into said relationships knowing the other person felt the same. I wasn't exactly sure how I was supposed to feel about that, but it almost seemed as if it took the pressure off. We could have fun tonight, I could lean in and soak up the evening, and so could Jacob.

Perhaps it would be a little stressful, maybe there would still be temptation and need and desire, but it wouldn't be nerve-wracking, wondering if one of us wanted something the other couldn't give. We had put all of our cards on the table, and now here we were, sitting together in a trendy little restaurant in Fort Collins—the epitome of farm-to-table—and I was starving.

"Oh, this is a tapas restaurant," I said, flipping through the menu. "I've always wanted to come here. Beckett said it was great, same as Archer, but I just haven't had the time. Or I haven't dated much," I added quickly, wincing. "Sorry, I was just telling myself I wasn't nervous, but now I think I'm nervous."

Jacob grinned at me and shook his head. "I was thinking that I wasn't exactly sure how tonight would go because I didn't know if I should be nervous. I like that we seem to be on the same page."

"I can't help it. It's a little stressful."

"I'm stressful?" he asked, teasing.

"Of course, you are. You know it. Don't act like you don't or aren't."

"Maybe," he said on a laugh. "So, Beckett and Archer have been here? Not Benjamin?"

I shook my head. "I'm not sure Benjamin has ever been here, but he's the quiet one out of all of us."

"Really?" Jacob asked, and it sounded like he cared what was happening with my siblings and me.

"Benjamin is a little more soulful as if he knows who he needs to be, but he isn't in the mood to tell anyone about it. Beckett, on the other hand, can be a little more growly, a bit louder. But when it comes to protecting each other, they sometimes switch roles as if they know that the other needs them to take their place for those few moments. Not physically, but at least who needs to be the rock and who needs to be the one who leans."

"I always found it interesting when we were younger that you and Archer were twins, same as Beckett and Benjamin."

I sighed and sipped my chilled white wine. "Yes, apparently, twins run in our family. There are many sets, and I think I saw triplets somewhere on my father's line, too."

"Triplet Montgomerys?"

"Yes, but not related to the Montgomerys you know down in Denver."

His brows rose. "Wait, what?"

"My mother's maiden name is Montgomery," I said quickly. "She is the younger sister of the older generation of Montgomery guys that live in Denver. You know her brother, Harry."

"Yeah, he went through some crap a few years ago, and I helped him with his will." I shook my head. "Thank God the family didn't need to utilize it then, but it was still scary."

I pressed my lips together, swallowing a lump of emotion. "My cousins went through hell with that, but Uncle Harry's doing just fine. My father is also a Montgomery, but from a line not related to the Montgomerys my mother is part of."

"That would be awkward," Jacob said dryly.

I snorted. "Tell me about it. I have cousins in pretty much every state it seems, and it gets a little complicated, so there's not a huge family reunion, but it's nice. I like knowing that wherever I go, I can find family. Even if we've never met or are fourth cousins twice removed or something like that."

"My parents were only children, and then they only had Jonah and me. I don't have any cousins, and I don't think I have any aunts and uncles in the second generation either."

"I didn't mean to make you sad," I said, reaching out to touch his hand.

"You're not making me sad. I find it a little overwhelming, but it's nice that you have so much family. My parents and I do okay, even though it's just the three of us now."

Unsaid was that one day soon, it might only be the two of them, but I wasn't going to think on that. After all, anyone could have their last moments on this Earth taken from them at any given time. It would be wrong to focus on what we could lose in the next breath rather than focusing on what we had.

That was something I had to remind myself often and was something I would have to continue reminding myself while I was in Jacob's presencea.

"So, have you decided what you'd like for tonight?" our waiter said as he came back to the table.

I winced. "I'm sorry. I haven't even looked." I scrolled through the menu again. "I have no idea."

"Are you allergic to anything?" Jacob asked, looking over the menu in front of me.

"No, but I'm not a huge fan of crab or shrimp."

Jacob let out a mock gasp. "Well, it's over," he said, and I laughed. The waiter joined in on the laughter, but there was a little nervous tension, as if he didn't know whether we were kidding or not. Since I was getting to know Jacob, as well, I didn't blame the man.

"They have a tasting profile here," Jacob began. "What do you think? It should be enough for two, right?" Jacob asked, and the waiter nodded. "That was what I was going to suggest. As long as you don't have any allergies, we can make this work easily for you. And you're both already drinking the wine I would have suggested for it, so we're winning there."

"That sounds wonderful, then," I said, handing the menu over. "Is that going to be enough?" I asked.

"I'm pretty sure you're going to have leftovers, even with tapas," the waiter said before he moved away.

"I don't think he realizes how hungry I am," I said dryly.

"Oh, I'm pretty sure we're going to eat every single morsel."

Jacob held up his drink, and I did the same with mine. We clinked glasses. "To taking an evening off," he said.

I sighed. "I love the sound of that. Although I do have to go to work tomorrow."

Jacob shook his head. "Really?" he asked.

We each took a sip of our wine, and I swallowed, letting the light pear flavor settle over my tongue. "Yes, we have a huge project coming up for the family, and many of us are still working on individual smaller projects, as well. It's a little time-consuming right now, and Dad wants us to come together to talk it all out, on top of our regular meetings."

Jacob frowned. "I thought that Beckett was the project manager, and Clay worked with him."

I played with the stem of my glass. "Yes. But our father is still technically in charge of it all. He doesn't have a title, other than to say he's the final authority on everything. After all, it's his family business."

I hadn't even realized the bitterness in my tone until Jacob's brows rose. "Really? Is that working?"

"Clearly, it's not. It was for a while, but since Montgomery Inc. down in Denver is doing so well and becoming known worldwide, my dad feels like we need to compete with them, even if we're not technically connected to them at all."

"That's got to be complicated."

"I don't even want to get started because I want to enjoy the evening and however many tapas show up on our table. Let's just say I'm going to have a hard week ahead of me."

"I have court most of the week, and one of my paralegals

is finally coming back from maternity leave after having moved up here with us, so it's going to be a tough week for me, as well."

"They moved with you?" I asked.

"Not everyone did. Some of them stayed with the old practice or found other jobs. I didn't require any of my staff to move with me. I asked, hoped, and it worked out. I got the best of the best, and I know some of them will stay long-term. Some will move on when the time is right, but we're making it work for now. I'm just a little shorthanded."

"I would offer to help you, but I'm not quite sure I know how to help with any of that."

"And it sounds like you're a little busy yourself," he said.

"Just a little," I joked.

Our waiter came back with the first small plates, and my mouth watered.

"Is that bacon?"

"Candied bacon, as well as a few other delicious items."

He started to explain our meal, and as I laughed and joked over small, beautifully presented plates of beef and chicken and sea bass with vegetarian options on crisp greens, and little pieces of fruit to whet our palate, I knew I might pass out later from gastronomic joy.

When we were through, we made our way back to Jacob's car, our fingers tangled, and I leaned against his shoulder. "You may have to lower me into your car. I'm exhausted," I joked.

Jacob turned then and pulled me into his arms, sliding his thumb over my mouth. I swiped out my tongue, and he grinned before lowering his face to mine, his hand moving to cup the back of my head. I moaned, kissing him back with the same ferocity he approached the embrace.

"I think I would do anything you wanted tonight, Annabelle. I'm yours to command."

I went wet at that and pressed my thighs together. The damn man knew what he was doing. "I thought it was just dinner and drinks tonight," I nearly panted.

"We both know that's not the only snack I'll be having tonight."

"You're about to fuck me on top of your car, aren't you?" I asked, laughing.

"No, because we parked under a light, and I'm not really in the mood to spend the evening in jail." His hands slid up my dress ever so slightly, and even though we were alone in the parking lot, I still shivered, wondering if anyone could see.

"I need you," he growled. "Watching you slowly taste and savor your food all night, your tongue constantly flicking out as you nibbled and sucked on everything you ate...I practically came right there. I didn't realize watching a woman eat and enjoy her food could get me hard, but here we are."

"Then I guess you'd better drive very carefully yet very quickly to get us home."

He kissed me hard on the mouth again, and then we raced to the car, laughing as we tried to put on our seat belts. Jacob barely remembered how to put the car in gear. It was only a five-minute drive, but I was breathing hard the whole time, and Jacob's hand was on my thigh, my skirt pushed up slightly, his fingers playing with my delicate flesh. He didn't touch anywhere inappropriate, and anyone watching wouldn't be able to see anything, but it was the tease, the knowledge that he would be there soon.

He pulled into his driveway, and we piled out of the car, both of us looking at each other, at our homes, and then we made a dash to his house, only because it was closer. I didn't care that any neighbor outside could see.

Jacob slammed the door behind us, and then my back was against the hardwood, his hardness pressed to my stomach. "I'm going to fuck you right here against this door. What do you say?" he asked, growling against me.

"I'm saying you're wearing too many clothes."

He kissed me again, a bruising force against my mouth, and then he pulled back, stripping off his black shirt and pulling it away from his body. It fell to the floor, and then he shucked off his shoes and pants in one go. Suddenly, he was naked before me, his body long lines of muscle and sinew. His dick was hard, a little moisture at its tip, and thick.

"Whoa," I whispered.

"And you, my dear, are wearing far too many clothes."

He came forward, and I gripped him at the base of his dick, pumping him once, twice. He groaned before tugging up my dress to plunge his fingers into me as he shoved aside my panties.

I let out a shocked gasp; my entire body clamping around him as I came at the first touch.

He pumped into me with hard, fast strokes of his fingers that pressed against my clit and the bundle of nerves inside me. I wrapped one arm around him, teetering on my heels as I used my other hand to dig into his flesh, reaching for strength and control.

I came again, never having orgasmed so quickly in quick succession before. And then he was pulling at the top of my dress as well as my bra, my breasts falling heavily into his hands. He lapped at my nipples, pressing my breasts together as he bit and sucked.

My hands were all over him, both of us needing, and then

my dress was near my feet, and I was kicking it away, still wearing my heels. Jacob lifted me by the thighs, and I wrapped my arms around his shoulders, needing balance. When he met my gaze, he plunged inside. There was no finesse, no soft touches. Just hardness inside me, and both of us panting. He pummeled me into the door, and I held on for dear life, moving with each stroke and still needing him more. I kissed him hard and raked my nails down his back. When he pushed even harder the last time, I came again and felt him filling me up, my name on his lips as he came.

He kissed me again, biting my lip, and both of us shook. He wore nothing, and I only wore my shoes, my heels digging into his skin.

"I am going to be completely marked up tomorrow," he growled, kissing me again.

"That's all your fault," I teased. "You're the one who had me keep on the shoes."

He looked between us, and I did the same, watching as he continued moving slowly, leisurely, pushing inside me again, his cock disappearing before he gently pulled out. I shook, the sight of us connected in the most intimate way possible, hitting me harder than I thought.

I wasn't supposed to feel this. I wasn't supposed to want anything more, but when I looked up at him, I knew I was in trouble.

Because something was there in his gaze, something he blinked away quickly as if he were as afraid of it as I was.

I didn't think, I just kissed him again and held him as if I hadn't seen. Pretended I didn't feel the same.

I did what I had to do.

I made believe.

CHAPTER 12

Annabelle

The next morning, I rubbed my temples and drank my third cup of coffee. I was probably teetering on the edge of a caffeine addiction, but I didn't care just then. Jacob and I had continued our evening using pieces of furniture in his house, and then I had fallen asleep, both of us passed out from exhaustion and bliss. I had woken up the next morning, my phone alarm scaring the crap out of me, and practically scrambled from his bed, neither of us talking, just nodding at one another since there was nothing really to say.

We couldn't get too serious—that would ruin everything. And he knew I had to work.

I hadn't been running from him. We had just ended our evening a little later than planned, and now we had work to do. I needed to focus on the mess in front of me, not the mess that was the rest of my life, thank you very much.

"Hi. Annabelle? I was sent in here with coffee as well as a stack of notes, but I don't know if you want more or not."

I looked up at the sound of Clay's voice and smiled. "I will always say yes to coffee. I was just thinking that I'm already on cup three. I think four is fine."

He looked dubious. "Maybe you should have some water."

"Oh, I have. I'm allowed one cup of coffee to every cup of water. It's the only way I can function. Otherwise, I start getting jittery."

Clay just stared at me.

"I'm fine, promise. You can ask the others."

"It's true," Beckett said as he came in and stole the coffee from Clay. "And I know Paige gave this to you on her way to answer the phone, but this is mine now," Beckett said.

"I cannot believe you just stole that," I said, standing up from behind my desk.

"Of course, I stole the coffee from the kid. He's my second. Therefore, it's my coffee."

"Clay is near our age," I said, shaking my head. "He's older than Paige."

Clay cleared his throat. "I'm older than you, too," Clay said, and my eyes widened.

"What?" I asked.

"I had to take a gap year, and then, with the kids, it took me five years to graduate. So, yes, I'm two years older than you."

Beckett just blinked. "That means you're only two years younger than me."

"Yep. So, not a kid. In fact, I've raised three kids. Maybe

I'll take that coffee," Clay said before Beckett took a drink, then grabbed the cup and took a sip himself.

I beamed. "Welcome to the family."

Clay smiled and shook his head. "You know, Storm introduced me to your family and welcomed me, and it's been crazy ever since."

"No, Storm introduced you to *his* family. Now you're with the real Montgomerys," Dad said from behind him, and I winced, shooting a look at Clay, grateful my dad couldn't see.

Clay gave me a tiny shake of the head, and I was glad to see he understood. I was honestly a little tired of the undercurrents when it came to my dad. And Clay didn't need to deal with this.

"We have a meeting?" Dad asked.

"Yes, but we're heading into the conference room for that," Beckett said, his voice low. He was doing his best to sound professional because we were at work, but I knew he was also angry. Dad kept wanting us to go over every single minute detail, even though we had already done so many times, and it was taking time and effort we didn't have.

I understood needing to be careful, wanting to be cautious, but it was even grating on *my* nerves, and I had more patience than Beckett did when it came to our father.

"I thought you liked to meet in offices, said it makes it a little warmer or whatever."

I shook my head. "There's a few of us today, and we'll all be more comfortable around a table rather than standing around my desk."

"Come on, Mr. Montgomery. I'll make sure you get the best seat," Clay said, and my dad shook his head.

CARRIE ANN RYAN

"I know where the conference room is. I helped build the damn place, didn't I?"

I sighed as my dad walked out, Clay behind him.

"I think Clay already needs a raise," I said.

"I think we all need a drink," Beckett grumbled.

"I wouldn't say no to a drink," I agreed.

Beckett narrowed his eyes as he looked at me. "I don't know. You look a little tired. Maybe you had too much to drink last night."

I blinked. "Excuse me?" I asked, keeping my voice light.

"Don't *excuse me*. I heard from Paige that you went out last night with Jacob Queen."

"You heard nothing of the sort," I said quickly.

"No, he stole my phone to check the weather—or so he said—and saw my text telling you to have a good night. I'm sorry," Paige said as she elbowed Beckett in the gut.

"I wasn't stalking, but my baby sister is going out on a date with the man who said he hated her. No, not going to happen."

I narrowed my eyes at him as I poked him in the chest with my finger. "First off, no, we're not doing this. You don't get to go all *big brother* on me. Second off, we're at work. We're not going to do this now. And if you make a scene in front of Dad, I will never forgive you. We're all dealing with enough right now. You know that. I cannot deal with his anger over his precious baby girl dating someone."

"So you *are* dating someone," he mumbled, and I narrowed my eyes. He held up his hands in surrender. "Okay, okay. Not here. But I reserve the right to hound you later, just like you hound me."

I shrugged. "Okay, fine. It's only right that we're even, I

guess." Not that I'd let him come at me again. I'd place myself strategically away from the office when the time came.

"Good, now we can get to work," Paige said, putting her hands together in front of her. "We have a lot on the docket today, and I have a feeling it's already going to be a *thing.*"

"Pretty much."

"Red alert," Archer said as he ran back to where we were standing.

"What?" I asked, alarmed, looking around for a fire.

"I accidentally moved my sleeve up a bit more than usual, and he caught the tattoo."

I scowled at him, my heart racing. "Archer. I know you wanted a half-sleeve, and it looks wonderful on your forearm, but you had to know that Dad would eventually notice the Montgomery Iris on your skin," I whispered, frantic now.

My dad did not like the Montgomery Iris. He didn't want his children to be branded with the other Montgomerys.

Archer rubbed his forearm and tugged his sleeve down.

"It's just getting ridiculous. He saw the ink, narrowed his eyes, was about to say something, and I kind of ran." The tips of Archer's ears reddened. "I know our dad is amazing and nice and a good person. It's just…he's not acting like it right now."

Benjamin walked into the building at that moment, saw the four of us huddled together in the corner by Paige's desk, and shook his head.

"What did you do?" Benjamin asked, running a hand over his hair.

"Well, Dad is double-checking all of our work again, saw Archer's tattoo, and is in a bad mood," I answered.

"And we left him alone with Clay," Paige added.

My eyes widened. "Crap. Clay's amazing, we can't have him quitting."

"Damn it. I've got this," Beckett said and stormed off, leaving us behind, shaking our heads.

"And you're late, bro," Archer said, glancing at Benjamin.

My brother shook his head. "It is too fucking hot for me to spend the coolness of the morning inside, dealing with Dad's plans, when I could be working on what I need to out at my sites. I get that Dad wants us to work on this as a family because he feels like this is his project, but I'm exhausted. My team needs me to be out there helping them, not in here in a nice air-conditioned unit, when they're out there sweating to death."

"I'm sorry, Ben," I whispered.

"I'm sorry, too. Now let's get through this meeting so we can get back to our real jobs."

"You know it's Saturday, right?" Paige said. "I mean, we all know it's Saturday. We're not even supposed to be working today. That was our deal as a family. That we'd take weekends off to protect one another and our staff."

"We know," the three of us said, and I sighed again. We made our way to the conference room where Beckett was glowering at Dad, putting his body between Clay and my father.

Clay didn't seem to mind. He had his chest out as if he were ready to stand up and protect us, as well. This infighting was ridiculous. It hadn't always been this bad. We used to go to family reunions, and Dad had gotten along decently well with his brothers-in-law.

But then the Denver Montgomerys got a little more press, made a lot more money, and while we were doing just fine, we weren't exactly in the same league as the rest of them—at least according to my father. I might disagree with that sentiment, but it wasn't as if I had a voice. Not really. My dad was just as grumpy about me wanting to do my own thing as he was about being compared to the people he always compared himself to.

"Okay, come on. Let's get this meeting going," Paige said and looked around the room. "Is Mom coming?" she asked, and Dad shook his head. "No, she went down south."

I held back a groan. Well, that explained the mood. Mom was visiting the new babies down in Denver or maybe in Colorado Springs. That meant Dad was alone at the house and grumbling about it.

And we were dealing with the consequences. I loved my father, I truly did, but sometimes he was such an asshole.

"Okay, let's get this shit on the road."

"Dad, language," Paige said.

"We're family here, and I thought you were all adults."

"We're in the workplace, and some of us aren't related to the Montgomerys."

My dad narrowed his eyes at Clay. "Fine, then. Sorry for the sentimentality."

I held back a groan. "That's enough of that," I said.

"Where are we on the up-keeps?" Dad asked, and Beckett rolled his shoulders back.

"We're where we need to be. The permits are either already in or well on their way. We are in different stages for certain areas, and some of our inspections are already complete. We're in a waiting game for team members as we finish a few projects, but we're doing well."

My dad narrowed his eyes. "We'll see about that. Let's go through it again."

I held back a groan, exhausted by all of this already.

However, maybe going through it for the fiftieth time would ensure that we didn't miss anything important. Or maybe it would just give me more of a headache, and I would cry to myself about it all later. I hated this feeling. The one that came from my father acting like a stranger. He asked so much of us, tried to take even more, and I knew he didn't understand us. But he was fantastic at what he did, and sometimes his pushing helped us in more ways than I could count. So, I would deal with this. At least, for now. If it got too bad, we'd have to think about it as a family.

I didn't have answers, but I was too tired to worry about it right now.

"What do you mean, you're not doing it?" Dad asked, and I brought myself back to what was being said.

"What I'm saying is, we decided to go in another direction," Beckett said slowly, and Benjamin met my gaze.

"What?" I asked, and he sighed. I hadn't meant to miss some of the conversation. Oops. *My bad.*

"You know the way we used to do things isn't as good for the environment. We're working on this plan. It'll be easier to add the solar with the layout we're moving on."

"You're just going to put it all out there then? Just change everything that we've ever done in this company?"

"Father," I said, keeping my voice stern but still respectable—at least as much as I could. "We've already decided to do this. You were in here when we did."

"I don't know. I still feel like it's too big of a change."

"It is a change. But it's for the good of the company. We all decided we needed to be more eco-friendly, and this is what we're doing."

"It costs too much," Dad complained.

"It does cost a lot," I said, agreeing with him. "Sustainability is something we all need to worry about. And so, we are. You agreed to this with us last month. And the month before. We're not changing this, Dad. I know it sucks, but we're going to do it."

Dad glared at me for a bit before nodding tightly. I knew this wasn't over. He'd complain again, and we'd have this same conversation at least once more. However, I was the architect. I was the one in charge of the plans that were leading us in our new direction. And Dad would have to step back eventually. I only hoped he didn't hate us when he finally did.

By the end of the meeting, my nerves were frayed, and we still had more questions than answers. Dad didn't quite understand what we were doing, that we weren't running away from his plans, that we were trying to build on them. And that was a problem. A big one. I just didn't know how to fix it.

"This is going to be a problem," Benjamin said as he walked in, echoing my thoughts.

"I think it already is," I whispered.

"We need to talk to Mom. She's the only one that can talk him down."

"Except she's getting just as bad as he is with some things," I said softly.

Benjamin shook his head, his eyes tight. "I don't have answers, and I know you don't either. But I hate this. I'm starting to hate that our parents still work here. And I like our family. I don't want to hate my parents."

"Ditto," Paige said from behind him, and Archer nodded.

Beckett just shook his head, glowering. "I sent Clay home. He took a Saturday morning off away from the kids to deal with Dad's shitshow. And I'm done. I don't know what we're going to do, but this isn't working anymore."

I met my siblings' gazes and nodded. "I know. We're going to have to figure it out. I just don't have answers right now. And I was going to work today anyway because I have plans to work on. I need to let my creative juices flow, and I haven't been able to recently."

"Because of Jacob Queen?" Archer asked, and I flipped him off.

"No, we're not talking about that."

"So, no plans tonight?" Paige asked, and they all looked eager to talk about anything but our family problems.

I just glared at all of them.

"I do not have plans tonight, other than to work. And maybe do this thing called relaxing."

"So, Mr. Fancypants hasn't even called then?" Beckett asked.

I blinked at him. "Did you just say fancypants?"

Archer snorted, while Benjamin just shook his head, his lips twitching.

Beckett shrugged. "I don't know. It just came to me. It doesn't seem apt now that I think about it."

"Okay, if this is where you want to be, fine. Since I left Jacob's bed this morning, I'm pretty sure we didn't need to make plans for tonight. If I see him, I will. If I don't? Whatever. It's not your business, any of you, and that's the last time I'll be talking about it in this building." I let out a breath. "Or ever," I added, as Paige's eyes widened, and my brothers just stared at me, mouths agape. "Out. Go do what you need to do. Stop bugging me."

"Where did you say you were this morning?" Beckett asked, his voice a growl.

"In Jacob's bed. Yes, I slept with Jacob Queen. More than once. And it wasn't even the first time. What are you going to do about it, Beckett? Are you going to beat him up? I thought you were all for your sisters being strong women who could take care of themselves. Are you going to be that kind of jerk?"

Beckett stared at me before his lips twitched just like his twin's. "You are a brat sometimes."

I shrugged. "Well, you make me."

"You won't even let me pretend to be all protective and glowering," Beckett said, pouting a bit. I loved my brothers.

"You're only allowed to be protective or glowering if someone hurts me. And only after they hurt me, and I ask you to help me. You don't get to take it upon yourselves to think that you know what you're doing."

"You're making this whole not-liking-this-guy thing very easy."

"You don't have to like or dislike Jacob, because it doesn't matter. We're just having fun." I hadn't meant to say that, and now they were all glaring at me again, including Paige. "Okay, that's enough. No more."

"It's not going to get serious?" Benjamin asked, tilting his head as he stared at me. "I thought sex would be pretty serious."

"When's the last time you got laid, Benjamin? You want to talk about that?" I spat.

Archer rolled his eyes. "Well, since we're talking about the last time hell froze over, we may need to sit down for a while if we're going to think about that long-lost time."

"You're an asshole," Benjamin said.

I sighed. "And this family is getting far too close. Go, do

your thing. We'll figure out the whole what-the-hell-is-wrong-with-this-family thing later."

"Whatever you say," Beckett said. "But if he hurts you, I reserve the right to hurt him."

"*We* reserve the right," Benjamin said, pointing at the three brothers.

Paige cleared her throat politely. "And *I* will be the one who helps castrate him. Do we not remember this?" All three guys winced.

I laughed. I couldn't help it. "I love you. Now go." Thankfully, this time, they did. I sank back in my chair, exhausted, even after all the coffee I'd had this morning.

Jacob hadn't texted, hadn't said we would see each other tonight, though I honestly didn't think we would. And that was fine. We didn't have plans. We didn't need them. I didn't want them.

At least, I didn't think I did. But the problem was, I didn't know *what* I wanted from him.

And that was something I would have to add to my long list. Later.

Much, much later.

CHAPTER 13

Jacob

"Remind me again what Paige's boyfriend's name is," I asked as I placed my hand on the small of Annabelle's back and headed into the restaurant. She turned to look up at me, a wry expression on her face.

"Colton. They've been going out for a few weeks now—or rather months, I suppose." She frowned, her nose wrinkling in that adorable way of hers. "I like him, but I don't know much about him. He came to a couple of Montgomery family events at the bar, and one Montgomery dinner where my parents did their best not to act as if they were excited that Paige might be settling down. However, I haven't spent too much time with him in a more intimate setting. I don't know much about him."

"Well, this should be interesting." I wasn't quite sure what I was supposed to say to that. I hadn't expected to be going on a double date with Annabelle's sister and her boyfriend, and from the uneasy look on Annabelle's face, she felt the same. Somehow, we had been bamboozled into this thanks to Paige. But Paige Montgomery was so sweet sometimes that when she smiled at you, suddenly you were sucked into doing whatever she asked.

"I am sorry. I didn't realize Paige was going to stop by the house when you and I were finishing up dinner last weekend."

I shook my head, kind of knowing that it wasn't Annabelle's fault that Paige had shown up at her house out of the blue. But when she had, she'd seemed far too into our casual dinner conversation, seemingly noticing things that weren't even there to begin with, and now...here we were.

"It's fine. We can handle this."

Annabelle studied my face, frowning. "I hope you mean handling Paige's questions and getting to know a guy I don't know, and not being out with me. Because this is still a double date. It does have the word *date* in it. That's not going to change."

As we entered the foyer, I shook my head, seeing people milling about as they waited to get to the hostess stand. I leaned forward and brushed my lips against hers. She sighed a bit, her shoulders lowering. "It's fine. I'm acting weird because this is different for me. I don't know Paige either. She was basically a baby when I moved away." Not technically, but it had felt that way years ago.

Annabelle snorted, her eyes dancing with laughter. "Oh, be sure to mention that after we sit down. She hates being the youngest of the family. And I mean of the entire family. She's the youngest cousin of our generation. Some are a full twenty years older than her at this point."

My eyes widened. "Oh. So, let me guess, you've been holding that over her head for years?"

"Of course. It's what big sisters do."

"Do you ever think she feels weird that she's not a twin?" I asked, not knowing why it came to me.

Annabelle shrugged and leaned into me as someone passed us. I put my hand on her hip and pulled her closer, the movement instinctual.

"Sometimes. But we don't talk about it much. She's still family. Still our sister. And I don't think Archer and I have that twin bond that others talk about. Sometimes, I feel like I know him better than anyone else. And sometimes he surprises me. But I guess that's the best thing about family—or at least one of them. Benjamin and Beckett, on the other hand, I feel like they're two peas in a pod, the opposite sides of a coin. Or whatever metaphor you want to use."

I snorted. "Okay, that makes sense. I've just never known a family with two sets of twins."

"I'm sure there's more out there, but we do like to be special, us Montgomerys."

"Why are we special?" a soft voice said from beside me, and I turned, Annabelle in my arms. Paige grinned at us, her dark hair pulled away from her face partially. A man with a chiseled jaw, bright eyes, red hair, and a mischievous smile stood behind her. "I don't know if you guys have met before. Colton, this is Jacob, Jacob, this is Colton."

I nodded. "We met at Riggs'."

"Yeah, sorry about that. At least I wasn't the one who hovered around you," Colton said.

I shook my head. "No, but I'm pretty sure the next time I see the girls' brothers, they're going to do the same thing to me."

"Probably," Paige said, bouncing on her feet.

"We should go and tell them we're here for our reservation." Annabelle looked around. "They seem busy tonight."

"It was hard to get a table for four," Paige said, nodding. "But Colton knows the chef, and I think that's how we got in."

"Let me go take care of it," Colton said before kissing the top of Paige's head and making his way to the hostess stand.

"Well, he's cute," Annabelle said, and I narrowed my eyes at her.

"Hey," I growled.

Paige laughed as Annabelle just rolled her eyes. "You're cute, too. I'm sorry."

"I have no idea why I put up with you." I laughed.

She grinned. "I do, but I shouldn't say it in front of my little sister."

"La la la, I'm not listening," Paige said, her hands over her ears.

I grinned then looked over at Colton as he waved us over.

"They're ready for us," Colton said, and Paige smiled up at him before taking his hand. I backed up so Annabelle could pass me and then followed.

The hostess started talking to Colton about something or other, and I figured he must know her, as well. She took us to a low table in the corner where we could see everything we wanted but still gave us some privacy.

"Thank you, Sandy," Colton said, and Sandy grinned and waved at everyone.

"Your waiter tonight will be Alejandro. He will be right with you. Enjoy your meal. It was so nice to meet you, Paige."

Sandy bounced off, and we all took our seats.

"You seem to know everybody," Annabelle said, and Colton shrugged.

"I come here often because I know the chef." He looked up at us. "We went to culinary school together. However, I went into the smaller restaurant-esque area. Not like Dave here. What he's done is amazing."

"I'm excited because I'm starving." Paige looked up at Colton. "Though I'm sure your food will be better."

Colton shook his head. "As I said, I only have a small bistro. We're opening a second one down in Denver, but I'm not going to be anywhere near this level. I like what I do and have, and it's my dream. I don't know if I could ever do something like this."

"I don't know, I think you could. As it is, you seem to make Paige happy," Annabelle said, and I wrapped my arm around her chair, giving her a look.

She just grinned and ignored me. I didn't know if we were here so Paige could grill me, or for us to grill Colton. But in the end, I was ultimately here for food because I didn't want to disappoint Annabelle.

How that had become a significant part of my day, I wasn't sure. I didn't want anything serious. I had enough on my plate. Even this date tonight cut into my work schedule. And Annabelle knew that and had even mentioned that we'd have to cut tonight short and head home early because both of us had meetings in the morning. Things we couldn't get out of. Besides seeing each other a couple of nights a week for dinner and for sex, if I were honest with myself, we didn't get to see each other all that often. We were both working, and we saw each other at my parents' house on the weekend, but that was it. We were playing things as casually as possible and not getting serious. Except for the fact that tonight seemed serious. It didn't matter that weeks had passed, both of us telling each other that this was just for fun and wouldn't mean anything. Tonight seemed a little bit too much for me. And from the way Annabelle kept glancing my way, I had a feeling she was on the same page. Or at least I hoped she was. Because I didn't want tonight to happen again. I didn't want to put expectations on her family or her that would hurt her in the end. We were having fun, letting off some steam, and that's all we could do.

I wouldn't let myself feel anything more because that would only hurt us both in the end.

And, fuck, I could not fall for my brother's widow.

That was the warning on a loop in my brain.

I could not fall for Jonah's widow.

They were just serving dessert when Annabelle looked at me and put her hand on my arm. "What's wrong?" she asked, her voice low as Colton and Paige talked to each other, smiles on their faces.

"Nothing, just thinking."

She frowned. "About what?"

"About what I'm going to do to you later before we call it a night," I lied and then leaned forward to gently bite her lip. Her eyes went dark, and Paige cleared her throat.

"Well, I assumed we were going to eat this chocolate soufflé, but I suppose if you need to go and take care of your dessert, you're welcome to it."

"Nobody is taking this chocolate soufflé from me," Annabelle said as she picked up the spoon. "Oh my God, it looks amazing."

"This one is pistachio with chocolate," Colton added, gesturing towards the airy green dough thing in front of us.

I had no idea how to cook, and I wasn't good at picking

out fancy foods, but everything in front of us tonight had been delicate and decadent. And dessert would be no different. We jokingly fought for the check, with Colton stealing the thunder from us in the end, having taken care of it even before we walked in.

"Sorry, I told you before, I'm handling this. Why do you think I needed to make sure I talked to the hostess before we sat down?" he teased.

"Well, I guess we'll just have to get it next time," Annabelle said on a laugh and froze ever so slightly in my arms.

I didn't even think Paige had noticed it, her eyes were so full of love and whatever other emotions filled her as she looked at Colton. But I *had* noticed that she had accidentally offered us up for another date.

Us, as if we were a real couple and not just keeping it free and easy. We needed to take a step back, figure things out. Or maybe I just needed to get my head out of my ass and walk away.

"Okay, you guys go enjoy your second dessert of the evening," Paige teased, and Annabelle laughed, her cheeks turning a pretty pink.

"You're terrible, and I love you." She kissed her sister's cheek and then hugged Colton. "It's nice to truly meet you and get to know you. And remember what I talked about earlier. I will hurt you," she said, even though she was laughing. I didn't think it was actually too much of a joke.

"You Montgomerys are vicious," Colton said and then met my gaze. "Don't you feel that? Are you ever afraid they're just going to attack you en masse if you screw up?"

I swallowed hard, doing my best not to look at Paige or Annabelle. "I think Annabelle and I know what we're doing."

Annabelle stiffened next to me once again, and I looked

over reluctantly as Paige gave me an odd look before blinking it away. "Okay, really, have a good night. We are going to have a good night of our own," Paige said, laughing as Colton picked her up in the parking lot and carried her like a princess off to their car.

"I would pick you up and carry you, but I'm super full," I teased.

"Oh, good, because I'm not really into the whole white knight routine."

Yet she was still watching them, a wistful look on her face. I gave a dramatic sigh, reached down, and picked her up. She let out a yelp and grabbed me around the neck hard enough that I nearly choked.

"I thought you said you weren't going to pick me up."

"You think I'm going to allow another man to outmatch me? Hell, he may know food and have connections, but I can act just as chivalrous."

"Okay, whatever you say, Jacob Queen," she teased and then leaned her head against my chest as I carried her to my car.

Hell, I was thinking too deeply. I needed to stop. This was wrong. I shouldn't want this. Shouldn't want *her*. But I wasn't going to stop. I couldn't. We got into the car and made our way to the house. Annabelle immediately pulled out her phone, frowning.

"What's wrong?" I asked, taking the ramp to the highway.

"Just looking at emails. One of the permits might not be coming through. Crap."

"Is that going to be a problem?" I asked, checking my rearview mirror.

"It's fine, happens all the time. Beckett's the one who needs to worry about it, same with Paige. However, we're all on the email loop, including Dad, so now I'm dealing with a hundred different threads. It's fine. It's just annoying." She put her phone down, closed her eyes, and groaned as she leaned against the headrest. "I'm exhausted and full, but tonight was a good night." She paused for a beat. "I'm sorry Paige was a little bit pushy. Colton, too. But I can't apologize for him because I don't really know him all that well."

"They weren't pushy." I paused. "They weren't *that* pushy."

Annabelle snorted. "They want everyone to be as in love and happy as they are. I don't think they realize that people can have other types of relationships."

She said the words very carefully, as if she were afraid that I would say something hurtful. Or maybe I just heard things that weren't there.

I was as jumpy as she was.

"So, are they really in love? Big *L* and all that?"

Annabelle shrugged, and I glanced over as she looked at her hands. "I'm not sure. We haven't talked about it. We do have a girls' evening scheduled, not that we allow ourselves to do that often these days. However, my friends Eliza and Brenna insist on it because I think they know Paige and I need a night off."

"That's good. So, you guys are going to talk about Paige?" I asked cautiously.

Annabelle snorted and patted my knee. I tried to ignore the heat, but I felt it anyway.

Damn it, I was getting in far too deep. I needed to push all those thoughts from my mind.

"We are probably going to grill her over Colton. Because I'm pretty sure there's the big *L* when it comes to the two of them. And Eliza's husband will be home from deployment soon. We're always worried about that."

"How long has he been over there?"

"Eight months. It was a long one this time. He's done a remote for a year at the beginning of their marriage before. But it feels as if he's been gone longer than they've been together," she said, frowning. "I don't know why I said that. Sorry. They love each other so much, and work so hard at their relationship because he's gone constantly. It just sucks for her. And I'm always worried.

"I get that."

"Anyway, they will probably ask about you. Only because now that I've gone out with Paige and Colton with you, she will have ammunition. And if she wants to stop us from talking about Colton, she will bring you up."

"You'll just have to keep the spotlight on her then."

"Yes, because some things should be private." She looked over at me quickly, and I reached for her hand. I squeezed it, and she smiled.

"Yes, I like that it's just the two of us. Others can think what they want, but we're having fun—you and me."

She smiled again, and I didn't see any hurt in her gaze, didn't see her flinch this time. Maybe I'd just imagined that things were weird.

"It's nice to have a night where I can relax with somebody, have some great sex, and then be all pumped for work the next morning."

I laughed and shook my head. "There you go, glad I'm good for something."

"I mean, I do appreciate your dick," she teased, and I laughed harder, practically shaking as I pulled into my driveway.

Her phone dinged again, and she cursed. "Crap, I need to handle this. It's Beckett." She looked over at me. "Raincheck?"

"Did you just raincheck me for sex?" I asked, laughing again.

"Yes. But I was just talking about your dick, and now I won't be able to ride it." She moved forward and gently patted my crotch as if she were patting my head. "I'm sorry, buddy. I'll be back soon."

I laughed again, gripped her neck softly, and kissed her hard on the mouth. "I'll take that raincheck. Now, go do your work thing. I have paperwork, too."

It would help me get her out of my system so I could focus on what was important and the plan we had in place. Me falling for my brother's widow was not part of that plan. She smiled one last time and scrambled out of the car. I watched her carefully as she made her way to her front door and walked inside. I let out a breath and made my way into my house, knowing I would need a stiff drink and a lot of work to pore over.

It would be a long night, doing my best not to think about Annabelle Montgomery. Only these past weeks, I had been starting to get used to having her on my mind and in my life more than not. And that should probably scare me more than it did.

CHAPTER 14

Annabelle

"Knock knock. I don't care if you're busy, we're here, and we have cheese," Brenna said as she made her way into my house, her key dangling from her finger. Eliza walked in behind her, rolling her eyes, her hands full, as well.

"You know, you could've rung the doorbell," I said, coming towards them to help alleviate some of the load.

"We knocked," Eliza said quickly. "But you didn't answer, and these are heavy."

"I'm sorry. Work."

"So we hear," Brenna said as we set everything on the kitchen island.

"Thank you guys for bringing everything over."

"You've been busy, and we know it. I mean, we're all busy,

too, but your days have been a little more hectic than most," Eliza said before she leaned down to kiss me on the cheek.

"I love you guys," I said and hugged them close. The front door opened again, and Paige walked in, grinning.

"Oh, I'm missing the group hug."

Paige had two bottles of Prosecco in her hands and a bag of groceries on her arm.

"I come bearing gifts." She set everything down near the rest of the things and then opened her arms. I laughed, and the four of us hugged again, leaning into one another.

"I'm glad we're doing this," I said.

"Oh, good. I was afraid we would have to push you into it," Paige said, hugging me hard as we started setting up our dinner.

"You shouldn't have to push me into anything. And I'm sorry I've been so busy with work."

"And Jacob, we hear," Brenna said, and I shook my head.

"No, you are not getting me to spill anything."

"Open the Prosecco," Eliza said, grinning.

"Yes, we're going to get her drunk, and she'll tell us everything." Paige clapped her hands in front of her chest and beamed. "I want to know it all."

"You are a dork," I said, laughing.

"Why am I a dork all of a sudden?" Paige asked, frowning.

"Because you're my sister, and you shouldn't want to know everything. It's weird."

"You don't need to tell me about the sex things. But you need to tell me about everything else."

I did my best to keep the smile on my face, but I didn't know why it hurt so much. Probably mostly because of what I had to say next. "Considering that it's only sex stuff between Jacob and me, I don't think I have much else to say."

Paige's eyes widened. "No, that can't be right. I saw the two of you at dinner. There was definitely more than only sex between you."

I shook my head, doing my best to deny it all.

"So, it's just a friends-with-benefits thing?" Eliza asked, sounding a bit disappointed. "I mean, not that I don't miss the benefits part of a relationship. I just thought with how much time you guys spend together it was something more."

I sighed and looked at my friends. "Okay, I'm not getting into this. We're here to talk about Paige and Colton. And hear what Marshall had to say when you finally talked to him," I said to Eliza, speaking of her husband.

"And you'll notice that I have nothing to give in terms of the gossip when it comes to men, but I am here to aid with all of my wise knowledge since I know what I'm talking about," Brenna said dryly.

I cringed. "And we're here to talk about work and life and all the shows I'm missing since I haven't been able to binge anything recently."

"It's because you've been too busy having sex with Jacob Queen to watch TV," Paige said, and I threw my hands up into the air.

"Okay, what are you watching?"

Paige blushed. "Well, I've been a little busy myself," she said and ducked as Brenna threw a piece of bread at her. "Hey, don't waste food."

Brenna scowled. "Fine, I won't waste food. But we are going to eat and enjoy ourselves. We can talk about sex later. Because since two of us in this house are not having sex, it isn't fair that that's the first thing and the only thing we talk about."

"Seconded," Eliza added. "And I'm hungry.

"I'm starving," I said, shaking my head. "I skipped lunch."

"I realized that." Paige glowered. "I tried to make sure you got fed today, but you were in and out of meetings all day. I didn't have an opportunity to make sure you ate."

"You don't need to take care of me," I chided.

"It's my literal job. I'm the office manager. I manage the office."

"And that includes me and my calorie intake?" I asked.

"If it has to. If my siblings and Clay don't take care of themselves, I will do my best to make sure that changes."

"I'm fine, don't worry about me."

Paige met my gaze, and something passed behind her eyes that I didn't quite understand. "I'll always worry about you. You are my big sister. My much older, yet not always wiser sister."

I threw another piece of bread since Brenna didn't have one in her hand.

"Hey, that is perfect French bread for the spinach artichoke dip I made," Eliza said and went to work setting up our plates.

"And it's amazing," Brenna said, her mouth full of it.

"Okay, we have the artichoke dip. We also have honey chicken skewers, rice bao balls, and a veggie tray," Brenna noted, going through her list.

"I brought meatballs, as well," Paige interjected, pulling out the Crock-Pot I hadn't realized was in her bag. "The little sweet ones that you just need to use a toothpick for."

"My mouth is watering." I looked at the feast in front of me.

"And I made cupcakes," Brenna said, pouting.

I laughed. "Why do you always pout when you bring over cupcakes?"

"Because I'm a cake decorator. Not a cupcake decorator."

"You love cupcakes. You love decorating them. You only get pouty when your clients want a mediocre cake and a thousand little cupcakes in a tower. That means they only want the cake as filler."

"First up," Brenna began, "my cakes are never mediocre, so you take that back."

I nodded, holding up my hands. "I'm sorry."

"You should be. And second, you're right. They want plain cake you can cut into and hide behind a curtain or something. And they want everyone to believe they're going to get a cupcake personally for themselves. But three hundred cupcakes in a nice little spiral to make a cake? It doesn't happen. Pinterest and insta-weddings and all of that stuff is ruining my business."

The three of us looked at each other and started laughing as Brenna puffed out her chest.

"Pinterest and Instagram and everything that's wedding hashtag related keeps you in business," I said dryly.

Brenna cringed. "Maybe. But the woman who came in today to discuss her wedding cake changed her mind—for the fifth time. Maybe I just hate cupcakes. But I made them for you anyway." She flipped the top of the box, and my mouth dropped open.

"Oh my God," I whispered.

"I needed something to do with my hands. So, we have a variety. Lemon and strawberry, chocolate gateau, and carrot cake." Each was immaculately decorated with perfect little individual marzipan and fondant animals. There were unicorns and pandas, and a small sleeping elephant. Each of them looked like a piece of art, and I couldn't wait to stuff them all in my face.

"You went circus on this?" I asked, laughing.

"My brain kept thinking of a hundred different things, so I went with cute animals. And I'm going to eat all of this dip so long as Eliza lets me. Maybe put a few balls in my mouth because you know I like talking about balls in my mouth," she said, and we laughed. "And then I'm going to eat that elephant."

"I don't know, the elephant looks amazing," Paige said as she reached for it. Brenna slapped her hand and pointed at us all. "No. We eat cupcakes after dinner. You know I usually like dessert first, but I'm in a mood, and you have to listen to me."

"You're not making any sense, but I love you." I leaned forward and kissed her on the cheek, and then we settled down with wine and our food.

The doorbell rang about thirty minutes into our dinner, and I frowned, looking at everyone. "Did we miss somebody?" I asked as I stood up.

"I don't think so," Paige said. "Maybe it's Jacob Queen."

I rolled my eyes. "He is working tonight. And he's in the office so he's not going to be stopping by."

"You know exactly where he is?" Eliza asked, beaming.

"Okay, enough of that." I looked through the peephole and frowned before opening the door. "Hey, Hotch, what's up? Anything wrong?"

Hotch shook his head and held out a big box. "I heard you mention it was girls' night tonight, and since I was in the neighborhood, I picked up some of those variety cookies from the bakery down the street. I know your friend Brenna makes the best cakes and cupcakes there is, but I figured why not add a little variety with cookies?"

I looked at him, smiling but a little confused. "You didn't have to do that."

"No, I didn't. But it was on sale, what can I say? I have a whole box for myself and the guys for later. I don't mean to intrude on your night, but I saw these and thought of you."

He handed over the box, and I opened the lid, holding back a groan at the sight of the perfectly iced sugar cookies. They were all pretty spring colors, each exquisitely done. I'd had cookies from this bakery before and had nearly fallen to my knees in gratitude for the delicious taste. I thought Brenna was a better baker, but that could be because she was my best friend. However, these cookies would be amazing.

"You honestly didn't have to, but thank you, Hotch."

He just grinned, put his hands in his pockets, and leaned back on his heels. "No problem. Well, I'm off to see the guys. I just wanted to see how you were doing. I haven't talked to you that much recently."

I leaned against the doorjamb, balancing the cookies on one palm. "I've been busy with work and family. You know?"

"And with your other neighbor, I hear."

He said the words lightly, and I didn't hear any jealousy in it. I was glad, even though I didn't want the whole neighborhood knowing I was dating Jacob—or whatever we were doing since we didn't actually want to be dating or anything serious like that. Hotch hadn't asked me out since Jacob came back to town. Not really. And he hadn't put on any moves or acted peculiar. The cookies he handed over hadn't been the first time he'd done something like that. He was just a nice guy, and I'd always hated having to say no to him.

The fact that he wasn't asking me out again or acting as if we could have something was nice—a change of pace.

"Well, it's mostly work," I said, cutting into any tension that might show up.

But there was none. Hotch looked happy. As if he hadn't asked me out a few times before this. Maybe I was over-thinking it. Perhaps Hotch was simply a nice guy who wanted to give me cookies. Delicious ones that I wanted to take a bite of immediately.

"Anyway, have a good night. Tell the girls hi. I'll see you later."

He waved, then headed back to his place, not even both-ering to invite himself in or wanting to see the girls. He was just a nice guy who brought over cookies. So why did I feel so weird about it? It was probably because, after so many times of gently saying no to Hotch, I said yes to Jacob after one day. That didn't make Hotch a bad person. It just meant that I wanted Jacob. Not that I could have him. Or want more than what we had. Because it wasn't serious, it couldn't be.

I closed the door and walked back into the living room. The girls glanced at me.

"Cookies?" Brenna asked, coming up and taking the box.

"Hotch dropped them off."

"Oh, right, they were doing that sale. Buy one, get one free, and the proceeds of any additional tips go to St. Jude's."

"Really?" I asked.

Brenna nodded. "Yeah, it's great. Marlene, the baker over there, is a wiz when it comes to cookies. We worked together on a few projects. And their sale today should bring in lots of donations and great business for her. I sent over a few, dare I say, cupcakes."

That made sense since Brenna didn't have a storefront

and worked on orders rather than selling directly to the public. She worked alone. She didn't need a store.

"That was nice of him," Eliza said, meeting my gaze.

"Hotch does things like that sometimes. He's never asked for anything in return. I try to reciprocate, but I think he's just a nice guy."

"Sometimes I feel like nice guys don't exist," Brenna said as she set the box of cookies on the table and sank down into the cushions.

"Sometimes they do," Paige said, smiling as if she were having secret thoughts about a particular person.

"Thinking of Colton?" I asked, pushing away any weirdness I felt. Just because I wouldn't have what Paige already seemed to have with Colton didn't mean I lacked anything. It just meant that I wasn't meant for that. I didn't need it.

I had been married once before, even if only in name. And I wasn't sure if I would ever want to do anything like that again. As it was, I barely had time for myself. I didn't have time for anything more serious than what was already going on.

"I think I love him," Paige blurted, and I smiled, pushing away all thoughts of Jacob. I sank down onto the loveseat with Paige and hugged her close.

"Really?" I asked, careful.

"Do you think it's too soon?" My little sister bit her lip.

I shook my head. "I'll never tell you what to feel. As long as you're happy. And Colton seems like a really good guy."

"You two went on a double date," Eliza put in. "So, you approve of him?"

"Not that she needs to approve of him," Paige said slowly.

"No, I don't need to, but I think I do. I mean, no one's ever going to be perfect for my sweet baby sister," I said on a laugh, and Paige shoved me gently. "But he seems like a good guy.

"He *is* a good guy. He makes me laugh. Treats me like a princess and an equal. And I need that. We're going slow, and I'm enjoying it. But I think I love him. I've never been in love before."

I looked down at my hands and frowned. "I haven't either," I said.

"So, not you and Jacob?" Paige gently prodded.

I laughed. "I told you, it's not serious. I like Jacob, but it's not the same as you and Colton. And I didn't love Jonah the way you love Colton. Jonah was my friend, and he became my husband in the end. To fulfill a wish. But it was for hope, not like you're feeling."

Eliza and Brenna knew about the marriage because the country did, at least our part of it. And I had told my best friends. They'd held me as I cried over it because I still missed the best friend I'd had before them. But they knew just as I did that what I'd had with Jonah had been friendship and hope to bring about a gentle peace, not what a husband and wife should have.

Paige turned to Eliza. "You've been in love before. I mean, you *are* in love," Paige corrected, and Eliza laughed.

"Yes, I love my husband. And I can't tell you what it feels like to fall in love. I just woke up one day and knew. It was as if I'd been falling every moment until the day I woke up and knew that he was the man I wanted to spend the rest of my life with. He was a little more headstrong about the idea of love," she said, and I leaned forward.

"What?" I asked. I didn't know the tale of how Eliza and Marshall fell in love. When I met her, she was already married, having moved here with her husband for his job.

"We met young," Eliza explained. "Not even eighteen yet," she added. "And he fell in love with me first. At least that's what he said, and I believe him. He always knows what he wants and goes for it. I take a little more time sometimes. That's how we fell in love. It's like this…knowing, this idea that the person you're with could be with you forever. Where you can't imagine yourself without them. And then, when you try to think about how it happened, or what your life could be like if you hadn't met them, you can't. It's this odd paradox where it doesn't exist in your reality. I just love him. And I miss him every day. I cannot wait for him to come home." Her eyes filled with tears, and since Brenna was closer, she held our friend.

"That is the sweetest thing," Paige said, taking a napkin to wipe her tears. I took one myself and dabbed at my eyes.

"I want that," Brenna said into the silence. We all looked at her, and she shrugged.

I smiled. "I've never had that, but I want that, too. Maybe one day. But I love that you have it, and that Paige might, too."

"Maybe," Paige said. "I think love is different for everybody, but I can practically taste the ideas you're telling me," Paige said. "I don't know if that's the right word, but you know what I mean."

Eliza laughed. "I know. It's almost tangible."

"Exactly," Paige said.

We began talking about love and futures, and I sank back, listening. I was happy, wasn't I? I had never had that feeling Eliza explained before, yet maybe that was a lie. Perhaps if I allowed myself to think about it, and what it would mean to have someone in my life like that, I would see a face.

And the fact that I was afraid I already knew who I'd see,

who I could already imagine myself allowing into my life, scared me.

Because I needed to be happy with what I had. I needed to focus on work and not take things too seriously. I needed to remember that I was already happy, and I didn't need anything else. And if I kept lying to myself, maybe one day I would believe it.

CHAPTER 15

Jacob

"*I* cannot believe that movie ended the way it did," Annabelle said, shaking her head as she leaned into me. I pulled her closer, and the two of us made our way through the park for our evening stroll after the movie.

"Well, it wasn't a romance. I think everybody was supposed to end up murdered. Or walk away sad. Apparently, it's art."

Annabelle looked at me and laughed. "Wow, look at you, sounding all snide and sarcastic if something doesn't have love in it."

I blinked, wondering where that train of thought had come from. "Not really. I was thinking that the movie was going one way, and they ended it weird and abruptly, probably because they didn't want it to be happy. Not that they needed happiness, but because they ruined the ending by trying to be subversive."

"I agree. I didn't expect you to see it that way. It's not like you read romance novels or like chick flicks."

I snorted. "No, not so much. But my mom loves them, so I'll never disparage them."

"You do, and you will not only incur the wrath of your mother but me, as well."

"I wouldn't want that," I said, teasing.

"Dinner was good, though," she said, moving away a bit.

"Dinner was great," I said, patting my stomach. "Of course, going from bulgogi and dumplings straight to movie theater popcorn probably wasn't the greatest idea. I don't have too much time to work out tomorrow with my deadlines."

"I'm thinking of either getting a standing desk, which I sort of already have with my drawing boards, or one of those little exercise bikes that go right under your seat. It can probably sit under my desk. I'll look weird during meetings."

"I wonder if Dustin could get me one of those. Of course, then he'd want one, and so would Seressia and Lucas, and we'd all be working out as we tried to get our briefs ready."

"Maybe it'd get rid of some of the tension. I know your job isn't easy."

I shrugged. "It's not like yours is."

She frowned. "I don't want to talk about work. It just makes me all grumpy and gets me thinking about my father, and I'm not in the mood to do that."

"Are you going to stand up to him?" I asked, not sure why I said the words at all.

"That's easier said than done. And, technically, while I

could stand up to him, it wouldn't matter all that much because I'm not the one who needs to do it."

"Beckett?" I said, frowning again.

"Yes. Beckett's the one who pretty much took over the job from Dad. And while Beckett does an amazing job and is brilliant, it's hard to flourish when Dad is always looking over his shoulder all the time, holding a grudge against people who aren't fighting back because they don't care."

"The other Montgomerys aren't at war with you?"

"Not in the slightest. The Denver Montgomerys..." She sighed. "Honestly, I don't even know if they realize my dad has a vendetta against them. It's so weird. He feels inferior to his brothers-in-law, my uncles, or something. I don't know, but it makes things so complicated, and it's not like we're even in competition with them. We're in different markets. And while, yes, I do talk to Storm, my counterpart in the company, we like being creative together. It's not like he's stealing from me, or I'm doing that to him. Beckett and Wes work together well, too. None of it makes any sense to me."

"I think you'll all be able to talk it out and move on some-day. But until then, it's going to be complicated."

"That's an understatement. It's already a little too much for me to bear most days. I don't like the man my father is becoming. And I don't like the idea that my mother stands back and lets it happen, even though it's her family."

"What about your father's siblings?" I asked.

She shrugged. "They don't live in the state, so we don't see them as often. But it's one big happy family—or at least happier than my dad with my mother's family. I hate that I can't fix it without yelling at my dad. And I don't want to be that person. Nobody wants me to be that person."

"I understand," I said and then reached out to tuck her

hair behind her ear. "Now, enough of that. We should probably get home soon. We both have early days." I looked down
at her then, and she smiled. Something twisted inside me.
Why was I doing this?

This wasn't what I wanted. Things were getting far too
serious, far too quickly. We would both end up hurt in the
end, and we were tarnishing Jonah's memory just standing
here with each other, pretending that we weren't thinking
about anything serious.

Or maybe I was thinking too hard, and we were both on
the same page. This had to be sex and us being friends.
Nothing more. And maybe even a whole lot less.

"Yes, let's get home." She paused. "I mean, to our homes."
She blushed. "You know what I mean."

I snorted. "Yes, I do. Come on." Suddenly, there was a
crack of lightning above us, and I looked up, then down at
her. We both laughed. Rain dropped down on us in a deluge,
pounding against our skin, splattering the pavement below
us, and bouncing back up onto our legs. I took Annabelle's
hand, and we ran towards the car, passing others as some
danced in the rain, and others ran with us.

"Was it supposed to rain?" she called out over the sounds
of the storm, and I shrugged, getting to the car first so I
could unlock the door. "I wasn't expecting it to, but it's
Colorado. Who knows?"

We both slid into the car, and I turned on the engine,
shaking my head. "This is ridiculous. Should we wait here or
drive through it?"

"Let me look on the app," she said and pulled out her
phone. She bit her lip, and I wanted to reach out and tug her
close, lick away the sting.

"Oh, crap. We're right at the edge of it, and it's only going to come harder and pound into us," she said and then burst out laughing. "I didn't mean that to sound so sexual, but here we are. I say we make it home. It's only going to get worse."

"You've got it," I said and pulled out of the parking lot.

The roads were wet and a little messy, but not too busy, thankfully. I had visibility out of the windshield, but my wipers were on full blast, and it was getting harder and harder to see as we got closer to the house.

Annabelle didn't say anything as she sat next to me, but she had one hand on the oh-shit bar, the other on her leg as if afraid to touch me. I only saw that at a glance when I turned, but I was glad I didn't have any other distractions because all I could do was focus on the road and try not to end up in the ditch. I pulled into the garage, grateful when it closed behind me, and turned off the car.

"Dear God," I said, finally letting out the breath I wasn't aware I'd been holding. My heart raced, and I shook my head. "That was ridiculous."

"We are drenched, and I feel like we just ran a marathon. My teeth hurt because I was grinding them. I was so afraid I might say something and distract you."

I leaned over, pulled her close using the back of her neck, and kissed her hard. "You're always distracting, Annabelle." I figured I should be honest. At least as much as I could be.

Her eyes warmed, and she grinned before leaning over to bite my lip. I growled and kissed her again. I nearly pulled her over onto my lap in the car but thought better of it.

"I could fuck you right here. Or I can fuck you in the house. You decide."

"I'm getting cold, let's go take a hot shower," she purred, and then she was out of the car, and I was following her, reaching for her as we made our way down the hall. My hand slid up her dress, her skin slick, and I plunged my fingers into her panties and inside her wet heat. She shook in my hold, letting out a startled breath.

"Foreplay," she gasped.

"I thought that's what I was doing." I crushed my mouth to hers. I worked my fingers in and out of her, my thumb rubbing her clit. Both of us were clothed, her purse still over her shoulder, and we'd only made it to the hallway. I needed to touch her. I needed to get her out of my system.

Because the sooner I did that, the sooner this would be about just sex—better for everybody.

I twisted my finger ever so slightly and pumped harder. When she came, I kept moving, and then released her before picking her up. She wrapped her legs around my waist, and we made our way to the bedroom.

Somehow, we were stripping each other out of our clothes, both of us tugging and pulling, and my mouth was on hers, then on her skin. I played with her breasts, needing to touch and to taste. She pushed me away slightly, and my back hit the wall of the master bath a second before she was on her knees in front of me.

"My turn first," she said and then licked the tip of my cock.

"I'm pretty sure you just came on my hand, so I was first," I said before I licked my fingers, meeting her gaze. "But you're always welcome to try and make it up to me." I tangled my free hand in her hair and pulled. Her lips parted, her eyes going wide.

"You want me to fuck your mouth?" I asked, my voice a growl.

She swallowed hard before leaning forward, both hands on

my hips, and swallowed me whole. She gagged slightly, and I pulled away before she hollowed her throat again and moved. I moved my hips with her, and we found a rhythm, her mouth warm and inviting and oh so good. I was about to come already.

But I didn't want to come down her throat. No, I needed to be inside her. Which was probably wrong of me, especially when I should push her away in everything that mattered. But that wasn't going to happen right now.

Instead, I pumped in and out of her mouth, her lips swollen around my dick. When I started to feel myself falling over the edge, I pulled away and tugged her up so I could kiss her hard again.

"Jacob, I want you to come," she whispered.

"I will, but it's my turn again," I said and then pulled her down to the floor, the soft bathmat under my shoulders. She fell on top of me before moving so she could rub her wetness over my dick.

I kissed her again, playing with her nipples, then slid my hand between us, grasping the base of my dick.

"You ready?" I asked.

She nodded, and then I cursed.

"Crap, condom."

She reached for the drawer nearest to her and pulled out the box of condoms she knew I stored there. I wasn't sure I liked that she knew so much about my house and where things were... Or the fact that I knew how she liked her coffee or where she stored stuff in her kitchen. But these were just condoms. This was only sex. She was making things easier for us by having things in reach. It wasn't changing things. This couldn't be serious.

She slid the condom down my length and then straddled

me again. I gripped her hips, met her gaze, and then she slammed home on top of me.

We both groaned, and she leaned forward. Since her breasts were right there, I licked one nipple and then the other before moving my hips, fucking her as she met me thrust for thrust.

When I needed a better angle, needed more, I turned us over so she was on her back, one knee near her ear. I slid into her again, pounding, thrust after thrust. I kissed her hard, her nails scraping down my back. When she clamped around my cock, coming again, I came with her.

We both shook, and I lowered her leg and then twisted so she was on top of me, no longer bruised into the floor. I knew I didn't actually leave marks on her, but that's what it felt like just then. As if both of us had moved too fast, gone too far. Maybe that was just what my subconscious thought.

Because this was becoming routine. This wasn't just sex. She knew things about me, and I was getting to know her more than I ever thought possible. And it scared me.

"Wow," she said before leaning on one arm and looking down at me.

"I guess we didn't quite make it to the shower."

She laughed. "We rarely make it to a bed, Jacob."

"Isn't that the truth? One day, we'll make it to a bed. Maybe." Perhaps a bed was too normal, too serious? Or, once again, I was overthinking things.

"Anyway..." she said, her voice trailing off. She met my gaze, and something flashed behind her eyes. Something I couldn't read. She looked vulnerable in a way I hadn't seen before. She moved off me carefully, and I rolled away to dispose of the condom. She swallowed hard and covered herself slightly as she bent to pick up her clothes. "I should get home. As you said, I have an early day tomorrow, and it's just easier if I'm home. You know?"

She was putting distance between us. I needed that, too, but there was something in her tone I couldn't read. Why? *Because you don't want to,* I reminded myself. I couldn't. If I read her as much as part of me wanted to, it would mean we had gone too far. And she would end up hurt. This was how it needed to be.

"Makes sense. Here, I'll walk you out."

"Jacob, I live right next door. I'm fine."

"I'd rather make sure you're safe."

Her lips quirked into a smile, and she shook her head. "I've lived here longer than you have, Jacob Queen. I can take care of myself. I always have."

She leaned forward, kissed me on the cheek, and then walked away, her clothes in hand as she made her way to the guest bathroom to change.

I stood, completely naked, still smelling of sex and Annabelle—and had no idea what the fuck I was supposed to do.

CHAPTER 16

Annabelle

I stared at my bedroom ceiling, knowing my alarm was about to go off at any moment. I should just roll out of bed and pretend I had slept. I'd maybe gotten two hours the night before, but it had been off and on when I wasn't tossing and turning. And I only had myself to blame.

I had run out of Jacob's home last night as if an ax murderer was behind me. I was so messed up. I couldn't believe I had run like that. As if the hounds of hell were on my tail. I just couldn't be in a room with Jacob any longer. And maybe that was the problem.

Because I loved him.

Damn it. I loved Jacob Queen. I loved how he made me smile, the way he made me laugh. How he could ask just the right questions when it came to my family to help me figure out what I needed to do—or even how I felt to begin with.

Eliza had been right. It hadn't been a single moment, but a series of them. I had found myself wondering who this man could be and how I could be with him, and now we were here. I couldn't take that back.

It couldn't change who we were or what we'd said about being in this relationship to begin with.

Yes, I loved Jacob Queen, but he could never love me. I had helped put that block on our relationship. Was right there with him.

So why did it feel like I had made a mistake?

Maybe the mistake was falling in love at all.

My heart hurt, and I rubbed at my chest over my tank top, wondering if I could make it go away. I wasn't supposed to love him. It was only supposed to be fun. Something entertaining, and a nice time to relax after a long day at work.

But now I was thinking about what kind of food he liked so I could choose a place for our next date. And what I would send to him for lunch at work. I also thought about Dustin, Seressia, Lucas, and the others on staff because I always sent them sandwiches along with Jacob's.

Because Jacob did the same for me.

He had sent a meal in for the office and my family just because he could. Because he knew we'd had a long day, and it would only get longer. And he just wanted to be a nice guy.

He hadn't even sent a note with it, saying he was thinking of me or anything romantic. It had been nearly business-like, and yet it had been the most romantic thing anyone had ever done for me.

I was losing my mind.

Because I couldn't fall in love with Jacob Queen. Only I was afraid I already had. I had broken the one cardinal rule of friends with benefits. I had fallen for the friend, and no benefits came with that.

My alarm finally went off, and I rolled out of bed, taking my phone with me to turn off the sound. I had to go into work today, face another family meeting, and try to get through this project without coming to hate my dad.

I didn't want to hate my father. He was just making things difficult these days. And what a horrible state that was. On one side of the coin, I was falling in love with a man I shouldn't. And on the other side, I was coming to hate the man who had raised me and taught me how to love my job.

He had been the first to show me architectural plans and walk with me through homes that he was working on to show me where joists went and what a support beam was. He'd taught me about shiplap and the design features he loved, and I too had fallen for it all. He had taught me so much, and now he was ruining it all with his bitterness.

I didn't know why it had turned out this way. Nor did I know what we were going to do about it. But something had to change, and soon.

If Beckett didn't do it, then I would. I might be the perpetual middle child of our group of five, but sometimes it felt as if I were years older than my family members. As if I had lived a thousand lives in their span of one.

But no, that wasn't right. They had each been through their personal journeys and hells over time. But maybe losing Jonah had changed things for me. My heart ached at the thought, and I gripped the bathroom sink, trying to steady my breathing.

I wasn't supposed to fall in love with Jonah's brother. I had married Jonah because he was my best friend, but I hadn't loved him.

Not the way I loved Jacob. And maybe that was wrong...
or beyond a mistake. But I didn't know how to fix it. I looked
at my reflection and wiped the tears from my face, annoyed
that I was crying over this.

I couldn't reconcile the girl I had been with Jonah with
the woman I was now with Jacob. Only I shouldn't have to.
Jonah would understand. He had never been the jealous type,
and he loved his brother. No, the more I thought about it, the
one thing I knew was that Jonah would understand my feelings for Jacob.

The problem was, *Jacob* wouldn't understand.

You have work to do, and that means getting over yourself.

I pushed away thoughts of Jonah and Jacob because they
weren't going to help anybody. Instead, I showered, did my
hair and makeup, and finished getting ready to face the day. I
loved my job, I loved creating, and I loved my family. But I
knew going into work today with my father would probably
be a bit too much.

The dynamics at the office were off, and I didn't want to
go in at all. I could work from home, but I wouldn't do that
because Paige was there, as were my other siblings. I didn't
want to lose my time with them.

I honestly didn't know what to do.

I made myself coffee in a travel mug, then headed out to
my car. I risked a glance over at Jacob's, but I couldn't tell if
he was home or not. He was probably already out for the
day. He worked long hours just like I did—sometimes longer.
He didn't have a group of friends, really. Though I knew my
brothers would probably invite him to something soon.
Either to interrogate him or because they were nice people
and knew that Jacob didn't really have any friends here.

"Annabelle," a familiar voice said, and I looked over to see

Hotch making his way out to his car. He had a travel mug in his hand, his work bag in the other.

"Good morning, Hotch."

"Good morning. Have a good day at work. Yay for coffee, am I right?" he said and lifted his mug.

I smiled, waved, and made my way back to my car. I could always count on Hotch to make me smile, even if there was no spark between us.

I made my way into the office and saw Paige already at her desk, phone to her ear, her fingers clicking away on the keys of her computer. She grinned, her planner outstretched, and her tablet next to her. She was in the zone. I just smiled, loving how my sister could tackle anything. She kept us all on our toes and in line, and I was grateful for it.

I went to my office, set my things down, and looked up as Archer walked into the room. He was a little more rumpled than usual, and I frowned.

"What's wrong?" I asked.

He glanced at me and snorted. "Wow, good morning to you, too. How much coffee have you had?"

I grimaced. "Sorry, you just don't have as much product in your hair, and you look like you didn't sleep all night." A lazy smile crossed my twin's face, and I shuddered. "Never mind, I don't want to know."

"What? I was going to ask why you have dark circles under your eyes. But, hopefully, it's for the same reason." I met my twin's gaze, and his smile faltered for a minute. "Shit. Are you okay?"

I lifted my chin and did my best to blank my expression. It didn't work. "I'm fine, and I had just as much fun as you probably did," I said. "And we're never talking about this again because it's weird."

"Very weird, but I love you anyway. You sure you're okay?" he asked, leaning against the doorjamb.

"I'm fine. Really. I just didn't sleep much. It seems you didn't either."

"I forgot my hair products at home, and I didn't spend the night there. Luckily, I had a change of clothes in the car, but I forgot the rest."

"So, you're not sharing a drawer then?" I asked, teasing yet wanting to know more about my twin's happiness.

"I do have a toothbrush at his house," he said, his smile widening. "I have a toothbrush. At my boyfriend's house. And he said I could just leave a couple of things over. In my own drawer."

Archer's smile became so bright, I thought astronauts in space could probably see it if he stepped outdoors. My heart gave a tug. "Really?" I whispered. "I'm so happy for you. You look happy."

"I am. Are *you* happy?" Archer asked. I blinked before putting a smile on my face. As usual, my twin saw right through it.

"Annabelle," he whispered, and I shook my head, tears threatening. Why was I even crying? Weird feelings. I needed to get over them. Just because I thought maybe I could love Jacob didn't make it real. He and I had an agreement. I wouldn't go back on that.

"I'm just tired. And I don't have the same kind of relationship you do with Marc."

"Okay, but I'm here if you want to talk."

"One day. Just not at work." I only said that because I knew I wouldn't be able to keep things from Archer for long. He always knew when I needed to talk, and I didn't know I needed to in the first place.

I knew he'd be there for me.

"Family meeting in the conference room, now." Dad's voice echoed from the hallway, and I frowned and met Archer's gaze.

"Is Clay here?" I whispered.

"He's off today, doctor's appointments and physicals for the kids."

"Good, because this is work. We don't do family meetings like the one that's about to happen when Clay is here," I bit out.

Archer rolled his shoulders back. "Good. It's about time we stand up to Dad."

I faltered, though I shouldn't have. "That's what we're doing? Standing up to Dad?"

"I sure as hell hope so. Because I know the strain on your face isn't just from what we're not talking about in your personal life."

I held back a curse, grabbed my tablet, and followed Archer to the conference room. I met Benjamin's gaze as he exited his office, his eyes stormy. No, today would not be good.

Beckett and Paige followed us into the conference room where my dad paced in front of the large desks, acting as the chairman of the board—or maybe a father ready to discipline his kids. This work environment was not healthy. Something needed to change.

"Sit down," Dad ordered. None of us sat. "What did I just say?" he asked, and I raised my chin.

"We're at work," I said, my voice calm. I felt anything but calm. "You're going to want to watch how you talk to us in our place of business. Anyone can come in at any moment to discuss plans, building… any number of things. What you're doing right now is not the face of the company we want to show the world."

"Don't act like you're infallible, Annabelle. You're one of the reasons we're in this mess."

"Excuse me?" I asked, my eyes opening wide. I did my best to ignore the barb slicing through my chest, but it was hard. This was the man who'd put me on his shoulders and handed me ice cream cones that would drip all over us. This was the guy who'd taught me to ride a bike and drive a car. And yet I couldn't see any of that in the person in front of me.

"No, you're going to want to step back, Dad," Beckett growled, moving past me. Suddenly, the five of us were standing shoulder to shoulder, with Beckett slightly in front, facing down our dad.

Hell, this was not how I wanted this conversation to happen, but I didn't know what else to do. I did not recognize the man in front of me right now, and I didn't know how to fix it.

But we had to.

Or we would end up losing something far more precious than our project.

"I was just on the phone with the McConnells," Dad growled out.

I blinked. "The McConnells? You mean the business that tried to outbid us for this project?" I asked, dumbfounded.

"Yes," he snapped. "The McConnells and I used to have an understanding. It seems we're going into more bidding wars with them because you don't understand how this business works."

"Excuse me, no. That's not how we do things," Paige said,

speaking up for the first time. Actually, it was the first time I had ever heard Paige talk back to our father.

"Excuse me?" Dad asked.

"I don't know what's going on with you, Dad," I began, but Beckett cleared his throat. I nodded, letting Beckett have this. At least, for now.

"Dad, why did you talk to the McConnells?"

"Because they bid on this project, too, and I wanted to know what they gave them. They weren't doing all this new-fangled shit that is costing us so much money. They're going about things the right way. We're going to lose out on projects if we don't follow that path. We almost missed a deadline with our permits, and we're already behind schedule. This is not the Montgomery Builders I created with my blood, sweat, and tears."

I froze, looking at the man. I couldn't believe what he was saying.

"*Our* blood, sweat, and tears," I whispered. "You might've started this with other people, but this building and everything in it came about because of your children. The adults currently looking at you."

"Montgomery Builders hasn't continued without good people behind it," Beckett added.

"No, we were all part of it. *Are* part of it. We each have assigned roles here, and we work together," Benjamin agreed.

"We're all in the positions we loved finding when we were children and teens and are now doing as adults," Archer added, and Dad just glared at him.

My dad still didn't like Archer's job, and I didn't know how to fix that. But this wasn't the time.

"And we didn't miss a permit," Paige said. "The county added an addendum, and that meant we had to redo the paperwork. That's on the county, and they're aware of it. We're not behind."

"I know how permits work, young lady."

"You can call me Paige," she said. "We're at work."

"And yet, none of you guys are working. You're running this thing into the ground. We're never going to beat Montgomery Inc. if we continue being lazy and don't follow the path I set us on."

"Your path got us here, but now we need to work together to keep going." I fisted my hands at my sides. "And stop comparing us to the other Montgomerys. They're not our competition."

"They are always our competition, damn it. Don't you see? They're looking down at us. They're acting all high and mighty because they have more money. Because they have more experience. Well, screw them. We will be bigger and better, and you'll just have to follow my lead if we're going to get there."

I honest to God did not understand the words coming out of my father's mouth. What was wrong with him?

"Dad," Beckett began, and my brother stepped forward. "No, this isn't going to be how it works. We are not in competition with the other Montgomerys. We did not lose a permit. We did not get behind on anything. All of that's wrong." I looked at my brother, frowning.

"See? You don't even know," Dad spat.

"No, we're behind on certain items because you keep having us triple-check things, and we have to show you in everything we do that we are adult enough to make our own decisions. You second and triple-guess everything we do to the point where I'm not even sure why we're doing this anymore."

"I'm the boss here. You're supposed to follow my direction."

"No, Dad. *I'm* the project manager. You are one of the owners of Montgomery Builders, but you don't lead. You sign the papers, and because you're my father, I've let you hurt our family with your antics, but I don't think I can do it anymore." Beckett stood his ground.

Tears threatened again, but I raised my chin, standing at my brother's side as we faced down our father. This was not how it was supposed to go. We were a family that worked together, played together, and loved one another.

And yet, it didn't look like that right now.

"So, you're just going to toss me out? After everything I did for all of you?"

"No, I'm going to be the one that does that," Mom said from the doorway, tears running down her cheeks, her hands shaking. "You need to come with me, Russell. Because if you don't let our children thrive, if you don't step away and realize what you're doing to this family, it's over. We're done."

I leaned into Beckett as my knees went weak at my mother's words.

"You're threatening to divorce me?" Dad spat, his face going ashen.

Mom looked down at her hands and let out a breath. Archer moved forward, and she met his gaze and shook her head. My twin stopped, and I reached out and took his hand. He squeezed mine hard, and the tears finally slid down my cheeks.

"I'm not threatening divorce, Russell. I love you, and that won't change. It hasn't all these years. But it's time to retire. It's time for us to move on and let our children thrive. I don't know what happened. I don't know why you hate my brothers so much. We're going to talk about that more later. But you need to stop. I love our children, and I don't want to lose them. So you and I are going to officially step down like we planned in the beginning. It's time you and I have some time for ourselves. And it's time for our children to be the next Montgomery Builders."

"Pamela, I don't understand," Dad whispered.

"Don't let your misconceptions about my family hurt ours," Mom whispered. She held out a hand. "Come, let's figure this out, and then you're going to apologize to your children."

"Not today," Beckett said. "You two talk. We can have a family dinner or whatever later and figure this out. But you're right. It's time to step down. It's time for Montgomery Builders to thrive, and we can't do that if we hate each other."

"I love you, Dad," I whispered. "I don't want to hate you."

My dad's eyes widened at that, and he looked at all of us as if seeing us for the first time. He swallowed hard. "Okay, okay. I don't know what's wrong with me."

"I think you love us, and you want what's best for us, but I think you forgot how to make that happen," I whispered.

"Come on now. You kids say you're adults. So get to work," Mom said, her voice shaky. "I love you all. We'll work this out. All of us."

And then they left, and I looked over at my siblings and just shook my head. "Did that just happen?" I asked.

"I think I need to sit down," Paige said.

Benjamin pulled out a chair as she sank into it. He kissed

the top of her head and then put his hand on her shoulder. "Well, shit," he said.

"I'm really glad Clay wasn't here today," Archer said, and we all looked at him. "I mean, we keep inviting him into the family, but this would've just been awkward."

I snorted, and then we all looked at each other and laughed, even though Archer hadn't said anything funny.

"What are we going to do?" I asked, looking at all of them once we quieted down. But I answered my own question. "No, I know what we're going to do. We're going to get to work, and we're going to be the best Montgomery Builders ever. Because that's what dad taught us. That's what we'll remember. And we're going to forget that Dad seems to have lost his mind."

"I just hope he means it this time," Beckett said, looking over my head at the empty doorway.

I reached out and hugged my brother. It took a moment, but Beckett hugged me back.

"I hope so, too," I said before I rose to my tiptoes to kiss his chin.

"Okay now, Mr. Project Manager. Let's get this shit done."

He grinned, rolled his eyes, and I somehow knew that everything would be okay. At least, with some aspects.

For everything else? Well, I didn't have any answers there, but I didn't need them. Not yet.

CHAPTER 17

Jacob

"Once again, I am questioning how I got talked into this," I said, looking over at Annabelle's twin. Archer just grinned and fixed his imaginary cuff. Considering that Archer had rolled up his sleeves, I knew he was only doing it to annoy me.

"Well, you were asked to come to the Montgomery cabal. And, here we are."

"We're at Riggs', a bar where I've seen you all before. Are we sure Annabelle and the girls aren't coming?" I asked, hoping they would be here later. I wasn't sure if I was ready for a guys' night out with the Montgomerys and their crew.

"Sorry, they have their own girls' night thing tonight," Marc said as he came up to Archer's side and slid his arm around his boyfriend's waist. Archer leaned into the other man as Marc kissed the top of Archer's head.

They looked happy, and I was glad. I didn't know Archer that well, mostly because I was doing my best to keep from getting to know the Montgomerys beyond what I already did, but since he was Annabelle's twin, I wanted him happy.

I didn't know what that said about me. Therefore, I wasn't going to focus too hard on it. I was allowed to want somebody to be happy without wanting anything more.

"Okay, they're all already here, that's good."

"Considering we met in the parking lot and you practically dragged me in here, are you sure they didn't all get here early so they could gang up on me?" I asked, not sure if I was joking or not.

Archer didn't answer, and that probably should have worried me.

"Over here, Archer," one of the twins called, and I narrowed my eyes as I studied them. It was Beckett. Although the two were identical, Benjamin was broodier, Beckett a bit angrier—at least that's what I could remember from back in the day. And now, for that matter.

"Okay, buck up, it won't be that bad," Archer said. I wasn't quite sure I believed him.

We made our way over to the corner, and I realized it wasn't only the Montgomerys at the table. A couple of other people I didn't recognize were there, but they seemed comfortable enough with the people that I *did* know. I figured they must either be cousins or friends. Annabelle kept joking about her family and the massive size of it. I wasn't sure which one this could be.

Beckett sat in the corner, Benjamin on his other side, and he tilted his head at me.

"Hey, you came," he said to me, and I nodded. "I did. As

long as you guys don't take me out back and make sure I never see the light of day, I'm here."

"We won't hurt you," Archer said as he put his hand on my shoulder and squeezed. Though he squeezed a little too hard, and I narrowed my eyes at him. He grinned innocently. I went to take a seat on the other end of the table and Archer took the spot near Marc.

"Jacob, this is Clay. He works with us down at the office," Beckett said, and the others nodded, waving at the man who seemed to be about my age. He looked exhausted. He had a kind smile and didn't throw *anything* at me for daring to date one of the Montgomery girls, so I counted that as a win.

Beckett continued, gesturing to the other man at the table. "And this is my friend, Lee. We rarely get him to come out these days since he works too hard. But here he is, in the flesh."

A man with dark hair, light eyes, and a grin that seemed to say he knew more than he was saying waved. "Hi, I'm Beckett's friend. Although most days, I try not to claim him."

Beckett just rolled his eyes and took a sip of his beer.

"Okay, I guess it is a guys' night and not a murder-me night." I took a seat on the other side of Lee, and the man just shook his head.

"I don't know. The night's still early. I hear you're dating my Annabelley."

I frowned at the nickname, ignoring his use of the possessive. "She lets you call her Annabelley?" I asked, scoffing.

Lee winced, and the Montgomery brothers laughed as Clay looked between them. "Not in the slightest," Lee said. "But you should try it. See how far you get."

Marc looked down at his phone and cursed. "I need to

take this. I'll be right back." He kissed Archer quickly and made his way out to the front of the bar as Archer watched him go, longing in his gaze.

"I do believe our little brother is smitten," Beckett said, and Benjamin snorted.

"Smitten?" Benjamin asked.

Beckett shrugged. "What, it's a good word. Smitten, like a kitten."

Archer just flipped them off. "Wait, I thought we were here to demand answers from Jacob, not me," Archer said.

My eyes widened. "Hey, just toss me under the bus a little harder, why don't you?"

"I thought that's what our plans were later," Lee teased, taking a sip of his beer.

"They're all very confusing sometimes," Clay said, laughing. "However, I don't think they're going to kill you. I hear the paperwork's a bitch. And you're a lawyer. You probably have friends with connections."

I met the man's gaze and grinned. "I do. And there are little notes everywhere saying that the cops should talk to a Montgomery if I ever disappear. Be warned," I said, and the others just laughed, rolling their eyes.

"Sure, whatever you say. However, why *don't* you tell us what your intentions are with our sister?" Beckett said, leaning across the table.

I gritted my teeth. "That's none of your business. And Annabelle would be the first person to tell you that."

"He's got you there. Remember when I tried to date little Annabelley?" Lee asked, and a little spout of jealousy seeped into me. I scowled over at the other man.

"You tried to date Annabelle?" I asked, my voice low.

Lee whistled through his teeth. "Not really. We nearly

went on a date just to piss off Beckett, but I would never do that to my best friends," Lee said carefully. "And it seems we don't have to ask too much about your intentions if you're already getting all growly at the mere mention of me almost fake-dating Annabelle."

"I don't remember this fake-dating thing," Beckett said, narrowing his eyes.

"I do," Benjamin said, sipping his drink. "You pissed off Annabelle while we were all in college, and she went to a frat party with Lee."

I scowled at the other man again.

"We went to the same frat party with our groups of friends. I did not go on a date or anything like that with Annabelle. Hey, why am I in the spotlight here? I thought we were here for Jacob," Lee said, and I laughed, shaking my head. "Enough of this," Lee said as Beckett started to question him again, although it was all good-natured. Even their teasing of me.

"For real, though," Benjamin said as everybody quieted down. "We're not going to hassle you over Annabelle, mostly because we're afraid of her, and it's her choice to date whoever she wants. However, if you hurt her, we will hurt you. Nobody messes with our sister." Benjamin's words were so calm, so infused with truth that I let a little fear slide through me, even as I narrowed my eyes.

"Annabelle and I know what we're doing. And if I hurt her, it'd be by accident. And I'm sure she'd make me pay all on her own."

"That's the truth," Archer said, leaning into Marc as the other man sat down again.

"Anyway, let's talk about better things. Like where is

Paige's boyfriend?" Lee asked, grinning. "I still haven't met that one. What's his name?"

"Colton," I answered, surprising myself.

"Colton. He sounds interesting. Is he treating our little Paigey right?"

"Paigey? Annabelley?" I laughed. "You need to do better with the nicknames."

"I tried to call her Strawberry Shortcake once, but it just took too long to say. I'll come up with something better to annoy her, don't worry," Lee said, grinning.

I shook my head, and then Riggs came up from the bar, walking directly to our table.

"Hey, lowering yourself to take care of us on your own?" Beckett asked, and Riggs just shook his head, pulling his hair back from his face.

"No, we're short-staffed today. Two of our people called in sick. So, I said I'd take care of the lot of you because you're exhausting. Tracy started the tab, but I'm here to help you with food."

Clay looked up at Riggs. "Can you make my check separate? That way, I can pay for my beer now. I need to head out. The kids are with a sitter, and I said I wouldn't be too late. We have story and bath time tonight, so it's going to take a bit." Clay pulled away from the table and reached for his wallet.

"I got you," I said, looking up at the other man.

"You don't have to do that," Clay said, his expression guarded.

"I don't mind. You're the only one who stood up for me a bit with regards to Annabelle tonight, so I'll buy you that beer."

Clay just rolled his eyes. "Okay, then put that beer on his

tab. And I'll get you later," Clay said, waving at the others. "I'll see you guys at work. Or around. Thanks for inviting me." Clay made his way out, and I didn't miss the fact that Riggs watched how Clay moved.

Well, that was interesting.

Riggs seemed to shake himself out of whatever he was thinking and smiled. "Okay, Montgomerys, and whatever other strange members have joined. Let's figure out what all of you are eating for dinner."

We ordered enough food for a banquet, another round of beers for them, and my first, and I leaned back and got to know Annabelle's brothers. It was complicated because they probably thought Annabelle and I had something more. We didn't. We couldn't. We would eventually have to figure that out because it would be difficult when the brothers—and Paige, for that matter—realized the truth of my and Annabelle's relationship.

Annabelle had told me I needed to come out tonight. Not to get to know her brothers for anything nefarious, but because she'd said I needed friends. I hadn't liked how close to the mark that was, but I was here, wasn't I? Getting to know people. Even if I was afraid that once Annabelle and I called it quits, her brothers would never speak to me again.

But that was something to deal with later. For now, I just enjoyed myself.

I was tired, and I didn't get to go out much other than with Annabelle, so by the time I got home, even though it wasn't too late, I was ready to fall face-first into bed. My phone buzzed, and I looked down at it, expecting to hear from Annabelle so I could ask how the night went. But it wasn't Annabelle. I froze before I quickly answered the phone. "Dad? What's wrong?"

"Everything will be fine. Your mom's just having a bad night. We're headed to the emergency room because we think she needs fluids."

"I'm on my way," I said.

"We've got this, Jacob. You have to work tomorrow."

"Then I'll be tired. I'm on my way. This is why I'm here, Dad. To help you."

"Okay." My dad paused so long that I was afraid he'd hung up. I held my breath. "It'd be good to see you."

"Okay, I'll see you soon."

We disconnected, and my hand shook. I reached for my keys again. I'd only had one beer and three glasses of water at the bar, so I was fine to drive, but all I wanted to do was reach for my phone again and call Annabelle, tell her where I was going.

But that wouldn't make sense. My parents would call her if they needed her. I couldn't call her and lean on her. That's not what we were. We were friends with a connection, sure, but I didn't want her to get the wrong idea.

When my phone buzzed again, the choice was taken from me.

Annabelle: *Did my brothers harass you?*

I cursed and got to my car, calling her on Bluetooth rather than texting her back.

"Hey. You're calling? What's wrong?"

"First off, everyone's okay. I'm just on my way to the hospital because Mom needs fluids."

"You're already in your car? Wait, you should've come and gotten me. I would have gone with you." I heard her rustling, and I cursed under my breath, just not loudly enough for her to hear.

"No, get some sleep. They're only going to let family back there anyway."

"I'm on their list as their daughter-in-law," Annabelle bit out. "Remember? I know this is hard for you...."

"You're right. So, I guess I'll see you there." She paused, and I heard so much in the silence. "We can talk about dinner with my brothers or something to make your parents laugh. They'd like that, right?" she asked, and I heard the fear in her voice. It echoed mine, but I tried to ignore it for both of our sakes.

"Sure. We can do that." I inhaled deeply through my nose. "We can do that."

"I'm getting in my car." She paused. "We should have gone together, Jacob."

"Maybe. I'm still trying to figure this out, Annabelle."

She was silent again, and I heard her car start, and the sounds as she pulled out of the driveway. "You're right. We're figuring it out. I'll see you soon." She paused again. "Jacob, she's going to be okay."

"Yeah, she will."

"Jacob?"

"Keep your eyes on the road, Annabelle. I don't want either of us to get into an accident tonight. I'll see you soon."

"Okay. I...well...bye." She hung up, and I gritted my teeth, taking the turn onto the highway.

Everything was so fucking complicated. This wasn't what either of us had wanted, and yet, here we were, going late at night to the hospital together to see my mother. I hated that I couldn't take away Mom's pain. There were so many things I couldn't do for her, but I had to find a way to help her however I could.

So, here we were, meeting at the hospital because my mother loved both of us. I'd almost said those words to Annabelle casually over the phone just now. And I was fucking worried that she'd almost said the same to me. But that wasn't what we wanted. Wasn't what *I* wanted. Something needed to change.

I didn't know how I was going to do it, not when change was the thing that inevitably crept up and smothered me these days.

Annabelle and I needed to talk, to get things situated. But first, I needed to hold my mom. And my dad. And I needed to remember why I was back in town.

CHAPTER 18

Jacob

$\mathscr{I}$ rubbed my temples and did my best not to scream in frustration. I didn't push everything off my desk and pretend that it would make it all go away. I didn't shout to the heavens and rage and confusion. Instead, I took a deep breath and searched my desk for water.

We had won the case yesterday, but I wasn't sure about my next one. I was so pissed off about everything, and it wasn't even about the defendant or the prosecution. No, it was about the fact that I couldn't focus. And it wasn't just one thing. It was a thousand of them.

"Jacob?" Seressia asked, walking into the room hesitantly. Seressia never walked hesitantly. But the fact she was, told me that I was likely scowling once again, something I didn't do before we moved here. Now, she was afraid of me. Damn it.

"Yeah?" I snapped. Even after that deep breath, I was still snapping. Today was not a good day.

"I wanted to see if you were okay. It's been a tough day, and with the internet down for those three hours, I know we're all a little behind. Can I get you anything?"

I closed my eyes and counted to ten. "I'm fine. Just get back to work."

"Okay, we can do that." She paused as Dustin whispered over her shoulder, and I opened my eyes to glare at them both.

"What?"

"It's your father. On line one. We're transferring it back."

I met Seressia's gaze, then Dustin's, and cursed.

After the incident at the emergency room, my entire family was on edge.

Annabelle and I had shown up separately to the emergency room, much to my parents' confusion, but we had both stayed long into the early hours of the morning. Annabelle had been fantastic and had studiously ignored me the entire time—probably because I acted like a bear with a thorn in its paw. Exactly how I was acting right now.

"Thank you, I'll answer it. When you guys are set with your to-do lists for the day, you can head home. I'm in a shitty mood, and I don't want to take it out on you."

"We're not in the best moods either," Seressia said. "Internet outages do that to a person. We'll be here for the duration."

I met Seressia's gaze, and she just lifted her chin. I gave her a tight nod. "Understood."

She left, and I let out another deep breath as I answered the phone. "Dad? What's wrong?

"We just got back from your mother's appointment. We

have a better picture of what we're dealing with. Can you come over later so we can talk about it?"

Ice filled my belly, and I swallowed hard. "Is there something I should know right now?"

"Your mother wants to see you. But we're okay. As okay as we can be." She paused. "Your mother's still here, son. Remember that. She's still here. And so am I. This isn't easy, but it is our life, and this is what we do."

Tears pricked the backs of my eyes, but I ignored them. "Okay. I'll be there soon."

"I thought you were working," my dad said.

"Well, I'm the boss, and I'm coming home."

Home. To the house that wasn't mine but was filled with my family. My home.

I thought about the other home I had, the one next to Annabelle. Our situation, or whatever the hell we had, was getting too complicated.

"Okay, she'll be glad to see you."

"I love you, Dad," I said quickly.

"I love you, too. And I'll see you soon."

He hung up, and I swallowed hard before looking down at everything at my desk. "Seressia, I'm heading to my parents'."

"Is everything okay?" she asked, Dustin on her heels.

I met their gazes, not knowing what to feel or say. They didn't know my family all that well, mostly because they hadn't lived here long enough to be able to get to know them. And it wasn't like I paraded my personal life in front of them all that often. Though between my ex-wife and us moving here for my parents, it seemed like I did more often than not these days.

"Everyone's okay. I just need to get over there to talk

about a few things. Thank you for taking up the mantle today. We'll get back to it tomorrow if that's okay. I'm going to take a few things home, but I think we all need some space and time away from this place." They kept staring at me, and I gritted my teeth. "Seriously. I'm okay."

"You're not, but you're going to work through it," Seressia said.

I snorted, a smile twitching on my face despite myself. "Well, thanks for that. And, seriously, thank you. All of you. I appreciate what you guys do, even if I'm in a shit-poor mood today."

"Well, you are our boss," Dustin said, coming up beside Seressia. "You're allowed to get all growly. We hide our moods better."

That made me laugh, and I shook my head. "Seriously, I'm heading out. But I'll have my cell on me."

"Tell your parents we're thinking of them."

I nodded at Seressia's words and then gathered my things.

I made my way to my parents' house, trying not to think. Trying to breathe. It was hard not worrying when everything seemed to be moving so quickly. I had moved to Fort Collins to help my dad, and that was what I was doing. Only some part of me hadn't let myself think of the exact reason I'd moved here.

"I can't lose her," I whispered, my voice cracking. My hands squeezed the steering wheel, and I let out a breath, grateful when I pulled into the driveway. I wasn't sure I should have been driving right then. I put my head back on the headrest and did something I hadn't done in far too long.

"Jonah, I miss you so damn much. I don't know what to do right now. You were my baby brother, and I always thought you'd be here, even when we knew life didn't always work out that way. But I can't lose Mom, Jonah. I'm not ready to say goodbye. And I know we have time, but every day seems to come faster and faster, and I don't know what to do."

My brother didn't answer. He hadn't before, and I knew he wouldn't. But just saying his name aloud, saying the words to him, seemed to help. Or maybe I was kidding myself. I needed someone to talk to. Needed to do something. And because Annabelle's face came to mind, I pushed that thought away.

No, talking to her about this would be too serious. It'd be too much. This wasn't what we were, wasn't what we wanted. I couldn't rely on her. Because if I did, then I'd love her, and I refused to love anyone else. Not after everything with Susan. Not after everything I was already dealing with.

There was a knock on my window, and I jumped before I looked up and saw my dad standing there, worry on his face.

"Hey, Dad," I said as I got out of the car.

"Hey. Do you want to talk about it?"

I clenched my jaw and shook my head, but I hugged my dad tight, leaning into him just a little bit. When he wrapped his arms around me and leaned against me even harder, I knew he was just as scared as I was. Jesus, I wasn't doing what I was supposed to do. I was supposed to be the pillar of this family—the strong one.

And I wasn't doing that. Things needed to change.

"Okay, I'm here," I said, my voice firm. "Tell me how you need me."

My dad met my gaze but didn't say anything. Instead, we walked into the house, and I did what I was supposed to do, I became the son I should have been before. The one they needed.

The only son they had left.

BY THE TIME I LEFT, I was a wreck, but things were okay. The doctor hadn't said anything different, other than that things might be more challenging for a little while longer. But my mother had laughed and smiled through it all, and I knew I would remember that laugh every time I got worried.

I pulled into my garage and did my best not to look over at Annabelle's house. I didn't want to know if she was there or not. Didn't want to talk to her.

I was so tired.

I walked into my house, set my things aside on the table, and went for a beer. I had work to do, thousands of emails and phone calls to deal with, but I just needed a moment. After, I would deal with all of it because that's what I did. I dealt with things. Meaning I needed to push aside things that were in the way and deal with what was necessary.

My doorbell rang, and I frowned, hoping to hell it was someone selling me something, because I didn't want to face anything or anyone else at the moment. I looked through the peephole, set my beer down, and held back a growl. When I opened the door, my ex-wife stood there, a small smile on her face, and flowers in her hands.

"Hi. One of Bob's friends said they saw you at the hospital while they were there getting stitches. I was worried about you."

That seemed like a very far-fetched story, but Susan knew many people and seemed to get information out of anyone. That's what made her good at her job.

"What is it you want?" I asked, my voice icy.

Her eyes widened. "I wanted to make sure you were okay. And I got these for your mother. I'm just so sorry that everything seems to be going downhill."

I narrowed my eyes. "Excuse me?" What exactly had she meant by that?

"Well, that's why you were at the hospital, isn't it?" Her eyes widened. "Oh, no. Was it you? Are you sick? Here, go inside. Sit down. Let me tend to you."

I blocked her from pushing inside. "What is this? What the hell are you doing here, Susan?"

"I miss you, Jacob. I'm just so sorry that everything happened the way it did, but I'm here now. I'm here to help. This must be so much for you, but I'm here."

I just looked at her, and then I laughed. Nothing was funny about this, but I couldn't help it, I laughed harder. "No, you don't get to do this. Just be with Bob, be happy. But this right now?" I said, gesturing between us. "It's never happening. I'm doing fine," I lied. "You need to go. You need to lose this address, ignore whatever reporter instincts you think you have. I'm done. Go now, Susan. Be well." She looked at me, her eyes comically wide, and then I slammed the door in her face.

Jesus Christ, I was done. Done with it all. I didn't want to deal with my ex-wife now or ever.

I chugged the rest of my beer, recycled the bottle, and thought about getting another one, then remembered the piles of work I had waiting.

When my doorbell rang again, the tension in my shoulders knotted, and I ground my teeth. I didn't bother looking through the peephole again, just yanked open the door and shouted, "What the fuck do you want?"

Annabelle's eyes widened, and she took a staggering step back, nearly dropping the brownies in her hands.

I cursed and reached for her and the brownies at the same time to keep her from falling. "Shit, Jesus Christ. I'm sorry, Annabelle. I thought you were someone else."

"Clearly. At least I hope so. I'm sorry. I was stress baking over work and everything, and I made a double batch of brownies. These are for you." She handed over the square tray and grimaced. "I'm not the best baker, but they're pretty chocolatey, and there's a ribbon of caramel in them, too. They're for you. I was trying a new recipe and thought you could use something."

She nearly turned, and I cursed again. "No, come in. Yeah, I think we need to talk."

Her shoulders stiffened, and she blinked at me before she gave me a small nod and walked inside. That probably wasn't the best way to start whatever it was I needed to say but yelling at her on my porch was likely worse.

"I would ask if you're having a good day, but I guess you already answered that for me," Annabelle said, rolling her shoulders back.

"Yeah, it's been a shitty day. My ex-wife just showed up right before you got here, and I thought you were her again. She won't leave me the fuck alone, and I have no idea what she wants. But I'm done with today."

"I can see that."

"I'm done with a lot of things, Annabelle."

She didn't do anything, didn't react at all, just stared at me.

I was already mucking this up. I might as well continue. "What we've had recently has been great, but it's been a little too much for me. We didn't want anything serious, yet every time I turn around, things are getting a little too tangled. I have too much on my plate to worry about anything else, so this needs to be it. We're moving too fast, and I'm done."

"You're done," Annabelle said, her voice steady, her face not showing any emotion. I had no idea what she was thinking, and I knew I wasn't doing this right. I didn't need to be a jerk, but apparently, I couldn't help it.

"I'm sorry, I know I should have done it softer or whatever, but we're friends, right? We can tell each other the truth."

"The truth," she repeated, her voice still devoid of emotion.

I looked at her and nodded, worry creeping up on me. Why wasn't she saying anything? "Yes, the truth. I have enough in my life to deal with right now. I don't need to complicate things further. I don't need anything getting in the way of my family and work. So, while what you and I had is nice, it can't happen again. I'm sure I'll see you around the neighborhood, and with my parents. But other than that, I think we need time apart."

I was saying all the right things. This was exactly what we both needed. I didn't want to end up hurting Annabelle in the end anyway. Because what if she fell for me? I couldn't be with Jonah's wife. That would be wrong. I was already doing a hundred things wrong. I didn't need to add to the pile. This was good. This was the best thing for both of us.

Annabelle just looked at me before she gave a small nod. The only indication she felt anything was a slight quiver of her lips before she thinned them.

I was an idiot.

"Okay. You said your piece, and I guess it makes sense. I suppose I'll see you around." Again, nothing in her voice. Not a single hint of emotion. "I wish you well, Jacob Queen. At least you don't hate me anymore." And then she moved past me, not bothering to touch me as she did. All I could do was stand there like a moron, like someone who had just made the biggest mistake of his life.

I wouldn't take it back. I couldn't. Because I was barely handling everything as it was. I couldn't handle any more.

CHAPTER 19

Annabelle

"$\mathcal{D}$o you know where we put the file?" I asked as Paige walked in, a frown on her face.

"It's on your desk. And it's also electronic, so it's in your inbox, all labeled correctly and tagged. You're just as anal-retentive as I am when it comes to files. What's wrong?" my sister asked as she sat across from me.

"I guess I haven't had enough coffee," I lied. I'd had four cups already and was a little jittery. But I wasn't sure what else to say. Nobody needed to know that I had fallen in love with the one person I shouldn't—the man who had once again broken me beyond measure.

I'd thought that it'd hurt when he hated me and when he had tried to push me out of his family's lives. But no, I had been wrong. This hurt far more than anything he could have said when he despised me. He'd pushed me away because it

207

was too much. I was that breaking point. I wasn't enough for him.

It wasn't fair. And yet it was the only thing that *could* be fair, right?

"It's not coffee. What's wrong?" Paige paused. "Is it Jacob?" she asked, her voice soft. My gaze shot to hers, and she frowned. "I didn't want to be right. Oh, no. I'm so sorry. What happened?" She paused again. "Wait, am I going to get angry? Should I go get the ball-cutting shears?"

"There are ball-cutting shears?" Eliza asked from the doorway, her eyes wide.

I groaned. "Why do we talk about castration so often in this office?" I asked, and then promptly burst into tears.

Eliza closed the door behind her, mumbled something to one of my brothers or Clay as they tried to get in, and locked the door. I found myself leaning on Paige as she came around my desk and held me close. And then Eliza was there, holding me on the other side.

"We're not going to castrate him," Paige said. "We may hurt him. But tell us what happened. I thought you guys were happy? That everything was working out?"

Eliza ran her hand over my hair and dropped to her knees in front of me so she could face me better. "What did he do?" Eliza asked.

"I feel so stupid for crying. I shouldn't cry." I sniffed, and then Paige handed me a box of tissues. I wiped my face and blew my nose, annoyed with myself. Eliza gave me my reusable bottle of water, and I nodded my thanks before gulping some down.

"That should help water down some of the coffee I know you have burning through your system," my best friend said.

I looked up at Eliza. "How did you know I'm jittery from coffee?"

"Because you're in pain and you want to do all the work you possibly can so you don't have to think about that pain. And when that happens, you use caffeine so you have all the energy to do what you're doing. And because I know you're not sleeping."

"And that's why you lied to me about needing coffee," Paige scowled. "I knew you were lying."

"Well, I'm not very good at it. Not even to myself." I sniffed again and wiped my eyes. "Or maybe I'm wrong. Jacob didn't seem to realize that I'm so in love with him, I feel like I'm dying inside. No, he pushed me away because I'm the straw that broke the camel's back. Or whatever other metaphor out there means being too much and yet not enough." I burst into tears again, annoyed with myself, but pushed away Paige and Eliza so I could wipe my face. "Sorry. I'll get it out of my system."

"You don't have to," Eliza whispered. "You can cry, you can scream, you can do anything you need to. I'm sorry you're hurting. I wish there were something I could do." She glanced over at Paige. "That does not include castration."

My sister winced. "I would never actually do it. It started as a joke, and now it's snowballed into this horrible thing. I wish there were a way we could help. Do we need to go over there and kick him in the shins?"

"I don't think that will help," I said and hiccuped before I blew my nose again.

"Did you leave anything at his house that we need to go get?" Eliza asked, her voice steady. That was Eliza, always so steady, even in the face of fear and anger and everything that went on with being a military wife. She was my constant friend. "We'll get it for you so you don't have to see him."

"I didn't. We're literally neighbors. We never had to worry about leaving a toothbrush at each other's house. We just did the walk of shame through our front yards."

"There was never anything shameful about what you did," Eliza said. "If he's making you think it was shameful, then that's on him." She paused again. "You love him?"

"I do," I said, annoyed with myself. "I didn't mean to. That's not what I wanted. We both told each other and ourselves that we only wanted to have fun, become friends, have sex, and not let it go any deeper. That we wanted nothing but great sex and conversation. And that's what we had. And then I was stupid and fell in love with him."

"There's nothing stupid about that," Eliza said.

"Seriously. You're allowed to love somebody. It's what we all want."

I met my baby sister's gaze and then shook my head. "It's not what I wanted. I didn't want that, and yet look at me. I'm sitting here, a weeping mess at work, and the brothers are probably ready to break down the door to get inside."

"It's not only your brothers," Eliza said, and I looked up at her. "Your father's out there, too."

I closed my eyes and cursed. "Well, should we let them in so we can give Jacob his last rites?"

"You don't *need* to tell them anything," Paige said. "In fact, don't. Let yourself do what you need to do. Grieve if you need to. And then later, we can kick Jacob in the shins. Because that's what I need to do."

I laughed a watery laugh. "Maybe that would help. But he has so much on his plate right now…"

"I know he does," Eliza said. "But he didn't have to hurt you."

"I wasn't supposed to develop feelings for him. It's my fault that I'm hurt. My fault that I fell in love with him. And my fault that he couldn't see."

"I might agree with you on the first two," Eliza said sharply. "But that's on him for being blind to your feelings. Or perhaps lying about his own."

I glared at her. "Jacob doesn't love me. He's been married before. He just got out of that relationship. He told me this was too soon, and we did our thing anyway. And now I'm going to have to see him and his family every Sunday for dinner. I just... I don't know what I'm going to do. I can't walk away from them. Yet Jacob's walking away from me."

The door opened then, and I couldn't say anything else. Still, I knew our conversation wasn't over. My father strode in, the brothers behind him. Clay stood near the doorway, and I waved.

"Hi, family member who's not an actual family member," I said to Clay.

"I'm just making sure you're not bleeding, and I don't need to call 911. Are you okay?" he asked, and all of the brothers and my father looked over at Clay, narrowing their eyes. They'd wanted to come in and try to save the day, but here was Clay, attempting to help.

"I'm fine. I needed a moment to cry about something that is none of anyone's business, but now I'm ready to continue my day without the drama. It's good to see everybody. Now, let's get back to work." I clapped my hands twice and stood up. Eliza and Paige cleared away the tissues, each kissed me on the cheek, and then strode out, pulling my brothers with them.

Beckett glared at Eliza, but he let her drag him by the arm, along with Benjamin when she got to him. Paige wrapped her arms around my twin and tugged. Archer just looked at her, rolled his eyes dramatically, and let her drag him out of the room.

That left me with my father.

"I'm not going to ask you if you're okay because I learned long ago with your mother that you'll tell me what you need to when you're ready," he said. It was an order.

"Maybe. I don't know when I'll be ready. But I'm fine. Just working on a few more projects."

I hadn't meant to say that last part since work was a touchy subject, but my father didn't wince. He didn't glower. Instead, he sucked in a sharp breath, nodded, and then stuck his hands into his jeans' pockets.

Jeans, as if he weren't coming to work in the office. I hadn't seen my father since the blowup, and I wasn't sure what to say now. Or if I should say anything.

"I wanted to say that I was proud of you and that I know I'm done. I'm officially retired. I came into the office to tell all of you that. And then we heard you crying, and now I want to know if I have to beat someone up."

I just blinked at him, trying to keep up. "I'm fine, Dad. Really. But are you?" I asked as I moved towards him. I stood in front of him, a bit hesitant, but he held out his arms. I wrapped my arms around his waist and sank into his hold, feeling like this was my father again, even if I wasn't sure what had changed exactly.

"I'm okay. I was stuck on an idea that I needed to be the one in charge, and I screwed up. I have a lot of atonement to do—a lot of things to work through, especially with Beckett...and Archer. And I will. But I wanted to let you know that I love you. I'm proud of you. And I trust you. And I'm sorry I was an asshole."

That made me laugh, and I looked up at him. "Well, I wasn't going to say anything," I said, and he narrowed his eyes at me.

"I can call myself an asshole, young lady. You watch your mouth."

"Whatever you say, Dad."

"Now, does this have something to do with that Jacob Queen? Do we have to teach him a lesson?"

I groaned. "No, everything's fine. Now don't ruin this special moment."

"I don't know. He may have to realize what happens when he messes with the Montgomerys." He paused. "Any Montgomery."

Tears pricked the backs of my eyes again, and I hugged him close, trying to pretend that everything was fine. That I wasn't still shattered inside. But this...*this* was one moment. One breath that was a little better. Maybe everything would be okay.

BY THE END of the day, I was exhausted but a little happier. Maybe I was broken inside and felt like I had lost a chance at something promising, but things were looking up. Work was good, family was good, life could be good.

I just needed to find a way to make that work without Jacob.

I was the last one out, as everyone else was either at project sites or done for the day. I had a couple of more hours left on a project, but I wanted to do it at home where I could be comfortable and put my feet up. That was the joy of working for my own business.

I was just about to get into my car when I heard the sound of screeching tires. I looked up to see a small sedan coming straight at me. My eyes widened as I saw a woman with a manic expression on her face, her hands on the steering wheel. At least that's what I thought I saw. I was too busy trying to get out of the way. I couldn't move forward, so I had to jump to the side. I fell to the ground, the car smashing into mine with the loud sound of twisting metal and the smell of smoking rubber. My head hit the pavement, and I bit my lip, blood pouring. I groaned, clutching my head as I tried to crawl away. Had the woman's brakes gone out? Had she missed the lane?

It couldn't have been on purpose.

"Damn it," a very familiar deep voice said from beside me. I looked up and frowned, seeing double, wondering if I was imagining things.

"Hotch?"

My neighbor sighed and bent down in front of me. "She wasn't supposed to hit you. She was only supposed to pick you up and bring you to me. But it seems I was right in coming to make sure she did it right. It looks like I should've done it myself. But she seemed a little dramatic. What can I say?"

I knew I had to be imagining things. It had to be a concussion. I couldn't understand it.

And then Hotch put something over my mouth, and I tried to scream. Only nothing came out, and my brain went fuzzy. The last thought I had was about the odd smell.

And then there was nothing.

CHAPTER 20

Jacob

I needed to get to the office before Annabelle left for the day. I knew she probably had a couple of hours yet at the drawing board unless she was onsite. I should have called her, should have waited until she came home so we could talk at her place. Only I couldn't wait.

And I couldn't even say that it had been a night's sleep that had finally cleared the cobwebs.

No, I had known that I had made a mistake as soon as she left my home, leaving me standing there as if I had just lost everything. And the problem was, I had.

I was such a fucking idiot when it came to Annabelle. I deserved anything that came to me. I shouldn't have lashed out. Shouldn't have pushed her away because I was scared.

I didn't know how I felt about Annabelle but watching

her walk away like that, so good at hiding her pain, I knew I would never forgive myself.

I had said some cruel things to her in the past, had allowed my fear and grief of losing my brother, of losing that time and control had twisted together inside me. I ended up hurting her. I knew I was still trying to earn forgiveness for that. And now I'd added more to it by being the asshole I was.

I did not deserve her forgiveness. Did not deserve Annabelle, period. But I was damn well going to try. I didn't know what I would ultimately do when it came to her, nor did I know what should be done. But hurting her like that had been cruel, and she deserved better. So, I would try to figure out how to accomplish that.

Even if it meant going into a place where her brothers and family were and prostrating myself at her feet. She deserved that. And more. Did I love her? I wasn't sure. Everything felt so different than it had when I was with Susan. And yet, had I loved Susan the way I should have? That was the problem, wasn't it? If I had to question it, maybe I hadn't.

I wasn't good at tasting the emotions that I was supposed to have—putting names to everything I was feeling. I was good at making plans and following through. And putting one foot in front of the other to fight for what I believed in.

That didn't mean I knew what I felt.

I let out a breath and turned down the street to where the Montgomery Builders offices were located. I didn't know if she would forgive me, but I at least needed to apologize. I had to try. There didn't seem to be anybody in the parking lot as I pulled in, and then my heart burst as I noticed the two cars left.

Annabelle's car, and another one, a very familiar sedan, crashed into the side of Annabelle's.

"Fuck," I muttered, and turned sharply, the sound of burning rubber loud as I nearly went on two wheels to get into the parking lot. I left the car running, barely remembered to put it into park and jumped out of my vehicle.

"Annabelle! Annabelle!"

I tried my best not to think about whose car was right in front of me. The one that had smashed into the driver's side of Annabelle's. The door was closed, and I couldn't see Annabelle anywhere.

"Annabelle!"

"Jacob?" a soft voice said from behind me, the voice filled with fear.

I clenched my fists and turned to face my ex-wife, who sat in her car, blood pouring out of a cut on her forehead, the airbag now deflated. There was glass all over the ground, and she looked to be in pain, but I wasn't sure where else she might be hurt.

But why the fuck was my ex-wife in this parking lot? Why had she hit Annabelle's car?

And where was Annabelle?

"What did you do?" I growled before I went to my knees beside her. She had another gash on her leg, and her knee was swelling. I cursed. "What happened?" I rasped.

"I got caught up in it. I didn't mean to. I was just supposed to scare her. Or get her to him. I don't remember."

My blood chilled. "Explain to me what the fuck you're talking about."

Another car pulled in beside me, its tires screeching, and then Beckett was shouting, another voice joining his.

"Annabelle!" Beckett yelled.

"I'm calling 911," the other voice said, and I finally recognized it as Clay's.

"What the hell?" Beckett asked as he came to my side.

"That's what I'm trying to figure out," I growled.

Susan met my gaze, her eyes a little unfocused. Shit. She had a concussion. I once thought I loved this woman. But if she had something to do with Annabelle being hurt, *if* Annabelle was being hurt, I didn't know what I'd do.

"Talk to me," I ordered.

Susan swallowed hard. "I missed you. I just wanted to see you."

"Who the hell is this?" Beckett asked, the anger in his tone palpable.

"My ex-wife," I gritted out.

"Where the fuck is Annabelle?" Beckett asked, nearly pushing me out of the doorway. I wasn't quite sure what Annabelle's brother would do to Susan, and I didn't need Beckett to end up with an assault charge or worse. So I stood my ground. But that didn't mean I wouldn't potentially throttle this woman to get answers. I let out a breath and glared.

"Answer," I ordered.

She met my gaze, tears spilling down her cheeks. "I was only supposed to surprise her so he could come and get her. I think. But then I saw her, and I just got so angry. I didn't even realize what I was doing." She let out a shaky breath. "My head hurts. But I didn't mean to. I don't think she's hurt. I didn't hit her with the car. She got hurt when she fell. She moved out of the way when I came at her. But then he took her. Jacob, everything hurts. Help me."

My hands were shaking, and I stood up, pushing Beckett slightly back. "Who took her?" I asked, my words clipped.

"What the hell is going on?" Beckett asked, his voice lower than even mine.

"Your neighbor. Hotch. We met when I came to visit you one day, and you weren't there. He was such a nice man. Said he was upset that you were dating his girlfriend, that you just took her. I didn't think that was right, but then I wanted you back, too, and it seemed like we had a common goal. I didn't know he planned to hurt her. And I don't know why I did what I did. I just got caught up in it all. It was a stupid mistake. Please don't call the cops."

"You're going to want to stop asking for things right now," Beckett ground out.

"Where is she?" I asked, trying to keep up.

Hotch? Annabelle's neighbor? The guy who kept trying to ask her out?

Dear God, it made no fucking sense. There was no way Hotch would do this. Would he?

I didn't know the other man, though, so maybe he would. And the other guy always seemed to show up at weird moments, was constantly watching, wanting to know more about Annabelle and me. But I'd always chalked it up to random curiosity, maybe a little jealousy. Not this.

"Where is Annabelle?" I asked, sirens sounding in the distance.

"The ambulance should be here soon," Clay said. "What are we doing?" the other man asked.

"I don't know where he took her." Susan started crying harder. I didn't move her in case she'd hurt her back, but I didn't know what else to do other than seething in front of her.

"Where did you two meet? Other than in front of my house," I asked, trying to connect the dots but failing.

"I don't know. It was just two places near here. He might've taken her there. I don't know. It wasn't supposed to happen this way. You were supposed to come back to me. You weren't supposed to leave me."

"I don't really give a fuck about you right now," I said. "Tell me the places you met."

Tears streamed down her cheeks, and I just glared at her, not sparing a single look of sympathy for her. This wasn't the woman I had married. Something had twisted her, and I hadn't recognized it. I would mourn that loss later, but first, I needed to find the woman I loved.

Because, Jesus Christ, I loved Annabelle. And nobody was going to stand in my way.

"I don't know. They were just small places we used to visit. In the woods." She rambled off two addresses, and Beckett tugged at me.

"You go to one. I'll go to the other."

"You need the cops," Clay said as if Beckett and I weren't making sense. Maybe we weren't.

"You tell them what's going on," I said to the other man.

"Beckett and I will go see what we can do. We'll meet the police there."

"Y'all are insane," Clay said but cursed. "But I agree with you. Because I'd do the same for my kids. Go. I'll keep an eye on her," Clay said, jerking his chin in Susan's direction, derision in his tone.

I met Beckett's gaze. I took one address and he took the other, and we left.

I knew the cops and the ambulance would arrive soon, and they'd probably want to question us. Hopefully, one of us would find Annabelle sitting and drinking tea with Hotch, waiting for us, and we could set the record straight with everyone.

Because if he harmed a hair on Annabelle's head, I'd kill him.

I couldn't lose her, not after I had just found her.

CHAPTER 21

Annabelle

My eyes blurred as I opened them, my body sore. I tried to get up, but I couldn't, my hands were secured behind my back. I pulled at my wrists, trying to lever myself up, but I was tied.

Why was I bound? And why did my head hurt so badly?

Bile filled my mouth, and I blinked away some of the blurriness, trying to process what was happening.

I was down on the floor, my legs tied, and my arms pulled tight behind me. I didn't know where I was. I didn't have a gag over my mouth, but everything felt like I was two steps behind, everything moving too slowly for me to fully catch up with what was happening.

Where was I? What had happened?

Flashes of the car coming at me came back, and I resisted the urge to scream. Someone had tried to hit me with a car, and as I'd dodged out of the way, I'd hit my head. And then Hotch was there.

Hotch with a funny smelling cloth, saying weird things I didn't understand.

Oh my God, Hotch had kidnapped me.

No, that had to be a dream, right?

And yet, here I was, lying on the ground, in pain. Tied up.

Hotch had done this? No, it couldn't be. Or could it?

"You're awake," Hotch said as he walked into the small room. He wiped his hands on a towel and tossed it over his shoulder as if he were a waiter in a restaurant. I didn't know why that was funny to me. Maybe I had a concussion.

Or maybe this is what hysterical felt like.

"What's going on?" I tried to say, and yet nothing came out. My mouth was too dry. I looked to the left of me and realized I must have thrown up before. Now, my hair was in it, and everything was gross. I didn't know what was happening.

"Well, shit, you got sick again. Don't know why Susan had to try and hit you with that car. She was only supposed to scare you. But then you had to go and jump and hit your head. You always were clumsy, Annabelle. It was why I was always there to help you around the house. Because you needed me. You always need me. And now we can be together. I'm sure you might need help, but that's what I'm here for. I'm always here for you, Annabelle. I just wish you would've realized it sooner. I had to move up plans, and I know you hate when things don't work out the way they should. But it's okay. I'll help you. Just like always. I will *always* be here for you." He emphasized the word *always*, and it scared me. Everything about this frightened me. I didn't understand what was happening.

"Hotch," I rasped, my throat feeling as if a hot poker had been shoved down it.

He clucked his tongue and shook his head. "Okay, let me get you some water. Don't know why you had to get so sick. You're just hurting yourself. But like I said, I will always be here for you. This is what I'll do for you. Always. Okay, let's do this." He left again, and I looked around, trying to figure out where I was, but I hadn't seen this place before.

Rugged walls. An old, wooden floor. It looked to be a small cabin in the woods or something. Not up to the mountains or the foothills, but near the city, maybe? I wasn't sure. I didn't know who was supposed to find me. I'd dropped my bag when I fell, and I didn't have my cell phone. I didn't have anything.

That meant I had to get out of this on my own. I needed to be my own knight in shining armor or whatever the hell those people were called.

I didn't know how I was supposed to do it, though.

I tried to wiggle out of my restraints, but they were tight. I thought it might be duct tape, but it was hard to move my head to check. I'd remembered seeing something on the internet. If I went down quickly with my hands spread as much as possible, I could maybe break through. But my hands were tied behind my back, so that meant I'd have to wiggle out, and I didn't think I was that flexible right now, not when every movement made me want to throw up.

That meant I had to get him to undo my restraints. Somehow.

"Here you go, come on, let me help you sit up."

I let him put his hands on me, let him help me to a seated position because doing it by myself had made me nearly vomit again. But every touch was revolting, and I knew I

225

would never be able to shower enough to get rid of this feeling.

I didn't want to imagine what might come next, what he wanted to do, so I pushed those thoughts from my head. The only things that mattered right now were getting out of here and protecting myself because nobody else would.

Hotch touched my face, gripped my chin a little too hard, and then put the glass of water to my mouth. I didn't know if it was poisoned, and at that thought, my eyes widened, and I pressed my lips together. He let out a long-suffering sigh, took the glass to his lips, and gulped some.

"It's not poisoned, Annabelle. I would never hurt you. Susan's the one who hurt you. Damn it. You're mine. We were always meant to be together. I don't know why you don't trust me." He shoved the glass to my lips again, and it clacked against my tooth. I gagged, and he poured water down my throat. I tried my best to swallow, but I choked, spluttering, spraying water in his face.

He cursed, tossed the glass to the side, and it shattered all around us.

A large shard fell behind me, and I did my best not to look at it so he wouldn't see where it had gone or that I'd noticed it was so close to me. Maybe that's what I would use to get out of the restraints. If I could figure it out. But I would, because I didn't know any other way to do this.

"See what you made me do? You're just so frustrating. You never did understand that I was supposed to be the person for you."

I swallowed hard, grateful I'd had some water, but I didn't want him to know how grateful I was. What else would I have to do for basic comforts? No, I wasn't going to think about that because I would get out of here before then.

"I'm sorry I didn't see you the way I was supposed to," I said, trying to think of the best ways to speak.

"You never did. I always thought you did, but you just liked teasing. Or maybe you were just too confused. We were getting somewhere. You were always kind to me; you were always mine. And then *he* showed up." Hotch glowered and sat back on his haunches.

"I'm sorry," I said, not knowing what else to say.

"Well, you will be," he warned, and ice slid through me to my soul.

"I hate him. But don't worry, once I figure things out, I'll take care of him, too. But for now, you and I will make sure we have exactly what we want. What we always should have had."

My fingers reached for the glass. I missed the first time, but I kept my attention on Hotch. "You were always good about bringing me baked goods, making sure I had everything I needed."

"Of course. I love you, Annabelle. I'm glad you noticed that I did things for you. Because it was always for you. All of this is for you."

I nodded, my fingers brushing the glass again. I felt a slice against my flesh, and I pressed my lips together tightly, holding back a scream. Blood welled, I could feel it sticking to my fingers, but I reached the glass again, this time gripping it as gently as I could. I did my best to work on the bindings as he spoke, as he told me every single little thing he had done for me. The treats, making sure I was always home on time. Because he watched me, he'd always watched me.

"When I built that gazebo out back? I could see right into your bedroom. Sometimes, you even left the windows open so I could see easier. You were so kind to do that. I love to watch you sleep. Though sometimes you had bad dreams. I wanted so badly to go in and protect you, but I knew I couldn't. Not yet. But now, anytime you have a bad dream, I'll be there for you. Always."

A shudder of disgust washed over me, but I ignored it. I kept cutting. Blood welled, and I knew I was cutting myself over and over again, but I could feel the bindings moving.

I wasn't sure how I would get my feet undone without him knowing, but maybe I could push him or cut him a bit. I didn't know if I had the stomach for that, but I had to figure something out. I couldn't sit here and listen to him talk any longer. Because he would run out of words to say eventually, and I didn't know what came next.

"I'm glad you were always there for me in case something happened."

"Of course, you are. Because we always wanted to be together. And you and I will be together forever. I'll make sure of it." He gave me a soft smile, and I almost cried, not knowing what he meant.

And yet, I was afraid I knew *exactly* what he meant.

"Okay, I'm going to go cook some soup for us. This is a cabin that my dad's friend owns. At least, one of them. They'll never think to look for us here. We'll have all the time in the world. But I can make some soup. Like I make so many things for you."

He leaned forward, brushed his thumb across my lips just like Jacob did, and I knew it was on purpose. I knew he had seen Jacob do that before, and I almost cried. And then Hotch leaned forward and kissed me hard on the mouth, nearly bruising me before he pulled away.

"I love you, Annabelle."

He didn't wait for me to say anything back. Instead, he left, presumably to the kitchen, and I let the tears fall. I tugged at my restraints, blood making the glass slippery, but then I was finally able to cut through the duct tape on my arms. I nearly cried out in relief. My hands were shaky, everything hurt, and I moved around to start on the bindings on my feet when I heard a noise out front.

"I wonder what that is?" Hotch said as he walked in.

I cut the last strip on my legs and rolled to my feet, ignoring the nausea, just as Hotch walked in.

"What the hell are you doing to yourself? Now I'm getting angry." Hotch came forward and picked up the gun on the nightstand I hadn't realized was there.

I shook, the shard of glass still in my hands.

"You couldn't just leave it be. No, you always had to be a lying bitch. You were meant for me, Annabelle, and now look at you, bleeding like a whore on the floor. Well, I'm going to teach you exactly who's mine. Because you *are* mine, Annabelle. You always will be. I'm going to show you how much." He lunged forward, and I lashed out, slicing his arm. He let out a shocked gasp and put his hand over the bleeding cut. The gun was raised to the ceiling, and I tried to crawl, but then he screamed again and pointed the handgun directly at me. I froze, and bile filled my throat again.

"I don't want to do this, but I will. Because there are other ways for us to be together forever. You should know that, Annabelle. You're meant for me."

And then the door slammed open, and I fell to the floor as Hotch whirled. Jacob came barreling through the door but froze when he saw the gun in Hotch's hands. Hotch reached down before I could do anything and gripped me by the hair, putting the gun to my temple. I froze, and so did Jacob.

"Did you tell him you were here? You whore. Of course, you did. You always opened your legs for him. You've ruined her, Jacob. You've ruined my Annabelle."

Jacob looked at me, his eyes wide, his jaw tense. "I was only checking to see how you two were," Jacob said. "I can see she's in good hands."

I wanted to cry in relief. I wanted to cry and rage. I didn't know what to do.

I just knelt there and looked at Jacob, wondering what would happen when the gun went off. Because Jacob would see this, and I would be gone. But Jacob would live forever knowing that he had walked in and the gun had gone off.

It had been Hotch, all along. But I knew Jacob would blame himself. But this wasn't his fault. It was Hotch's.

"I'm sorry," I whispered. "Jacob's here so I could tell him it's over," I said. "Really, Hotch. It's over between Jacob and me. You don't have to hurt him."

"Lies," Hotch spat.

Jacob held up his hands, nodding. He risked a small glance at me, and I saw the pain there, the worry, the...everything. My heart ached, but I could barely breathe. "No, I understand. It's over. She's yours, Hotch. You don't have to hurt her."

Hotch sneered and then moved the gun, facing Jacob rather than me. I nearly cried out.

"Well, if I don't have to hurt her, then maybe I should hurt you."

I looked up at Jacob, at the glass in my hands, and knew what I needed to do. I mouthed, *I love you*, and then I moved. I slammed the glass into Hotch's thigh. Hotch screamed as I pushed him away. Jacob moved then and reached for the gun in Hotch's hand as I pushed Hotch down, Jacob coming at us.

Hotch moved to shoot at me, but Jacob was quicker, but let out a sharp gasp as the gun went off.

I screamed, shoved Hotch down, and crawled to Jacob as Hotch started to cry, clutching his leg. Blood pumped from the wound, and I was afraid that I'd hit an artery. I couldn't care right then, though. The gun was in the corner, well away from Hotch now, but Jacob was on the floor, and I could barely focus, my vision going fuzzy around the edges. Jacob held his hip, blood seeping between his fingers. I looked down at him, tears falling.

"No," I whispered. "No."

And then there were sirens, and people shouting, feet slamming onto wood. Somehow, Beckett was there, too, pulling me away as the paramedics came for Jacob. I just whispered, "I love you," but I didn't think he heard.

I couldn't focus. I fell into my brother's arms, wondering how he could possibly be there.

"Save him," I whispered. "I love him."

Beckett held me close as the paramedics came. "We will, baby girl. We will."

And then I closed my eyes, and I prayed.

CHAPTER 22

Jacob

I felt like I had been run over by a truck. In reality, that had been Annabelle the week prior. I was home now, and I hadn't seen her since.

I'd wanted to, but between the police questioning, surgery to get the bullet wound on my hip fixed, and Annabelle needing time alone with her family, I hadn't seen the person I needed to see.

But at least I was home.

Maybe not at the home I currently resided in, but the place my parents lived.

"You know, you could head back to your place. Probably tomorrow if you want," my dad said casually as he came forward with a bowl of soup in his hands.

I looked down at the soup and licked my lips. "I don't know. If you're going to cook for me, maybe I should stay."

Dad rolled his eyes, even as tears welled up. I cleared my throat and patted the couch next to me.

"You know, I offered to get up and cook myself," I said.

"And I said if you stepped foot in that kitchen and put any weight on your hip or leg, I'd beat you. So, here we are."

"You two are so sweet to each other," Mom said from beside me, and I just looked over at her and smiled.

We were having lunch as a family, albeit not the same as it had once been. My parents had sounded so scared when they heard about the shooting. They'd made their way to the hospital despite my protests, but they had been there. Sat with the Montgomerys as they waited to hear about Annabelle's concussion and the cuts on her hands and arms that she needed stitches for. I hadn't seen her. It seemed everybody else in the world had seen Annabelle, but I hadn't.

I was trying not to be bitter about that.

"The soup tastes great," I said after a moment and looked up at my parents.

My mom was crying again, and I set down the bowl on the tray in front of me so I could reach over and hold her hand. I ignored the twinge in my side as I moved, and my mom quit crying immediately to scowl at me.

"Don't you dare hurt yourself trying to comfort me."

I smiled softly, even as my dad pulled me away so I could straighten. "I'm going to do everything I can to comfort you and to take care of you. Both of you. Just sidelined for a minute right now. I'll be fine."

"You scared us," Mom said, tears falling again. "I can't lose another son. Do you understand that, Jacob? I can't lose anyone else."

This time, tears pricked the backs of my eyes, and my dad gripped my shoulder, squeezing tightly.

"We can't lose you, Jacob. You're our son," Dad whispered. "We love you. We're not ready to lose you."

"I'm still here. I'm not going anywhere."

"But we almost lost you," Mom said.

"I couldn't let Annabelle get hurt," I said simply, although nothing about this was simple.

Tears fell harder, and my mom nodded as my dad stood up to help her wipe her face when she couldn't.

"And we're so grateful you did. Because she's our daughter. We love her so much."

I let out a breath, "I love her, too," I whispered.

"We know," my mom said as Dad gripped her hand softly. "We know."

"I don't know what's going to happen. We didn't end things on good terms before Hotch took her."

"This will probably change things," Mom said softly. "Hopefully, for the better. Because you two would be so good for each other."

"Even though she was Jonah's first?" I asked, not sure what I wanted her to say.

"She was Jonah's friend, confidante, and helper. But she's your fate. I believe that," my mom said, her voice steady.

I looked at my hands, the soup now cold. "I don't know what's going to happen next, but I'm going to fix it. Somehow."

"Of course, you are," Mom said before Dad and her met gaze.

"I hear Susan took a plea deal," my dad said carefully, and I closed my eyes and groaned.

"Yes, and I'm glad that it's not going to be any worse for her than it needs to be. Though I'm not sure what I'm supposed to think. My ex...I loved her. I would never have guessed that she could do something like this. What kind of man does that make me?"

"You do not get to put her decisions on your shoulders," Dad warned. "She made her choices, even while you were married. And that's why you two are no longer together. The fact that she went after our Annabelle, well, I don't even want to think about it. But, she did it, and now she's paying the price."

"And that asshole neighbor of yours is paying a steeper one."

Hotch had survived the nick to his artery, though barely. And he had a long road to recovery. And an even longer trial. I had already gotten word that his lawyers were attempting an insanity plea, but I was a damned good lawyer. I might not be part of the trial, but I knew the system. And the Montgomerys had a lot of connections around the state. I didn't think Hotch would get what he wanted. After all, he hadn't yet.

I would never forgive myself for not seeing it sooner. But none of us had. None of us had known.

And if I were ever alone with Hotch again, it's likely he wouldn't survive the meeting.

"You're getting all growly again. Let's not think about Hotch," Mom said quickly. "Is your office doing okay without you?"

"You know I'm still working here," I said dryly.

"Yes, we know, even though you're supposed to be taking it easy," Dad chided.

"Maybe," I said, shrugging, ignoring the twinge I felt again. "I'm not working too hard. Both of my staff members who were on maternity leave are back, and we're making do. I can't go to court, but we can get everything else done from where we're at. And the cases that needed to go to court right away are with another lawyer I trust here. Actually, I think we could probably work together well in the future."

"A partner?" Dad asked.

I shook my head. "No, but at least a confidant. It'd be good to have someone when things get too tough—someone who understands. But I'm not ready yet to make any decisions. I'm just glad that I'm here to make them later."

Mom started crying again. "So are we."

The doorbell rang, and I looked up, frowning. "Did you order something for delivery?" I asked.

"No, but it could be anyone," my dad said as he got up from the chair next to Mom and headed to the door.

"I love you," Mom whispered. I looked over at her again and reached out to grip her hand. "I love you, too."

"Now sit straight before your dad gets angry," Mom said, and we both laughed. And that was the image that Annabelle must have seen when she walked in, her face pale but looking so much stronger than she had the last time I'd seen her, passed out next to me as the paramedics worked on both of us.

"Annabelle," I whispered and tried to get up off the couch.

My dad cursed and came to my side.

"I will help you stand up, but you're only allowed up for five minutes. Then, you need to sit down again." My dad helped me so I wouldn't hurt myself, even though I thought I could have done it on my own. I just moved too quickly for Dad's liking.

Dad looked over his shoulder at Annabelle. "I'm putting this on you, young lady. Because we both know that he'll never listen to me."

CARRIE ANN RYAN

"I'll make sure he sits down before the five minutes are up."

"Narc," I said on a laugh, and then just stared at her.

"It's good to see you," she whispered.

"It's good to see you..."

"Well, I can see we're not needed," Mom said on a laugh.

Annabelle blushed. "I'm sorry, it's good to see you two again, as well."

"And we'll see you soon for dinner," Mom said as Dad wheeled her out.

"Did she mean tonight? Or on Sunday?" Annabelle asked, staring at me.

"Why not both?" I asked, swallowing hard. "Hi," I whispered, not knowing what else to say.

"Hi," Annabelle said back as she moved forward.

"I missed you," I said, not wanting to hold anything back. Not anymore.

"I missed you, too," she said as she stood in front of me, so close I could feel the heat of her. I reached up and pressed my thumb against her lips. She moved back, flinching.

I cursed. "I'm sorry."

"No, I am. Hotch...Hotch must have seen you do that before, and then he did it to me."

I growled, anger bubbling up. "If I see him, I will kill him," I ground out.

"I think you're going to have to stand in line behind the rest of my family," she said on a sigh. "And everyone will have to stand behind me."

"Let's not talk about Hotch anymore," I said, not knowing if that was the right thing to say at all.

"I don't want to talk about him either, other than to say that while I thought I was doing an okay job of saving

238

myself, I'm so glad you showed up. Beckett told me how you figured it out, about everything. I'm just so glad that you were there."

"If you thank me for saving your life, I'm going to get angry," I growled.

"Well, you'd better stay angry," she said softly. "Thank you. Thank you for being there, thank you for always being there. I'm so sorry you got hurt."

"Not your fault. And you don't get to thank me again. You're the one who made sure he couldn't shoot me in the chest."

"And you're the one who ensured he couldn't shoot me in the head," Annabelle said, and then her eyes widened as she put her hand over her mouth.

I shook my head, a grim sense of humor sliding over me. "What the hell is wrong with us?" I asked her.

"I don't know, but I don't want to think about it anymore."

I held out my hands, and she slid hers into mine and stepped forward.

"My five minutes are almost up," I whispered.

"Then I'd better be quick," she said.

"I love you," I whispered. "Always. I always have. Maybe just as friends before when we were younger, but it's turned into something more. And I loved you when I told you to leave. I was wrong. I'll never forgive myself for that."

"Don't. No more anger or pain over what would have or should have been. We can't do that to ourselves. Not anymore."

"Okay, then. Let's think about you and me. I love you so fucking much." Her eyes filled with tears, and I cursed. "Don't cry."

"I'm going to cry, and you can't stop me. Because I love you, too."

"I don't know how that makes sense," I said on a laugh. She rose to her tiptoes and kissed me softly. I cupped her face, grateful when she didn't flinch, then kissed her again, both of us being so careful with each other.

"Marry me," I whispered, shocking even myself.

She blinked at me, moving back. "What?" she whispered.

"Marry me. I love you so fucking much, Annabelle. We've already been through the worst together. I want you in my life. For now and always. I know it's too soon, I know it's insane, but I want you as my wife. I know you married my brother before so you'd be marrying into the family again, but we love you, Annabelle. All of us. I want you to be a Queen in truth."

She blinked away tears and looked at me. Out of the corner of my eye, I saw my parents in the doorway, both of them wide-eyed as they stared, love in their gazes.

"It's too soon," Annabelle whispered, and I tried not to let the blow show.

"Okay, but still be with me," I whispered.

"I'm not finished yet," Annabelle chided. "I love you. It's too soon. But yes, yes, I'll marry you."

I nearly fell to my knees, and when my dad scowled, even as his eyes were filled with happiness, I let Annabelle help me to the couch. Then she leaned over and kissed me softly.

"I love you, Jacob Queen."

"And I love you, Annabelle Montgomery, soon to be Queen."

And then my parents were there, and we were all smiling, and I knew that we had a long ways to go. This wasn't our end, it was only the beginning.

I looked up at the ceiling for just the barest moment and whispered a word of thanks to Jonah for bringing Annabelle into our lives.

And I knew he would be there with us always, too.

Even if it had taken me a long time to realize that.

CHAPTER 23

Annabelle

I leaned against my twin's side as Archer wrapped his arm around my shoulders and kissed the top of my head. While I wasn't much below average in height, it had always bugged me that Archer was so much taller than me. After all, we were twins and should at least be alike in some aspects, fraternal or not.

"Why are you scowling at me?" Archer asked, a single brow raised.

"Just annoyed that you took all the tall genes."

He threw his head back and laughed. The others in the room eyed us, curious gazes on their faces. Marc stared at Archer as if he were the only thing in his universe, and it made me so happy. Archer was happy with the love of his life, as I was with mine. Somehow, we had both found our happiness, nearly at the same time. It made me so happy that Archer seemed to have found peace as I had.

"Marc is looking at you right now like he could lick you up," I said, teasing.

Archer choked on his beer after he had taken a sip.

"Thank you for that image. You're my sister. That's gross." He paused. "But you know Jacob's doing the same to you. Now I need to scowl at him all big-brother-like."

I elbowed Archer in the gut, and he laughed. "I'm the big sister. Remember? Five minutes before you."

"Like you ever let me forget. You are seriously the middle child sometimes."

I beamed. "Am I? Or am I just the best?"

"Why are you giving yourself delusions of grandeur over here?" Beckett asked as he strode over to my other side.

I wrapped my free arm around his waist and leaned into his massive chest. "I'm allowed to imagine that I'm the best every once in a while. But since this family dinner is for Jacob and me—mostly me—I can pretend I am the best."

"And when our littlest sister decides to get married, do you think we'll have the same type of party?" Beckett asked, his voice low.

I glared at him before risking a glance over at Paige and Colton.

They were talking in hushed tones in the corner, both of them smiling at each other as if they were the only two people in the world. If they weren't careful, though, our father would go over there and drag Paige away by her hair, just because he could. Not because he didn't like Colton. We all liked Colton.

"Why are you standing over here ignoring everybody?" Benjamin asked as he came slowly to our sides. He gently shoved Beckett out of the way so he could hug me closer. Beckett just sighed. Archer opened his arm and grinned. "It's okay, big bro. Come over here, let me hold you."

Beckett made a show of it and then went over and hugged Archer so the four of us were in a line, all cuddling and watching Jacob's family, my parents, and the rest of our friends and family enjoying their dinner.

It wasn't a true engagement party, more like a proposal party as I liked to call it.

A proposal and a thank-God-we're-alive party.

And it had only been a few weeks since the kidnapping and shooting, so while I wasn't nearly okay yet, I was much better than I had been.

We had more things to worry about, far more things to deal with. And we would. But for now, Jacob and I were fine, as was the rest of my family. We had made strides in our largest project to date, and we were working as a cohesive unit. We were doing okay.

And I was marrying the love of my life.

I smiled. I couldn't help it. Before I could say anything, three kids, ages five to eleven, chased each other around the house and interrupted my thoughts. Archer laughed and then moved away so he could pursue them.

Clay, their cousin/dad/caretaker, ran after them, giving us all an apologetic gaze. "Sorry, they decided to play tag. In the house. Because this is my life."

I laughed, and then Benjamin pulled away to join in on the fun, surprising me.

"Well, it's good to see Benjamin out and about and smiling."

I frowned, looking up at Beckett. "What do you mean by that?" I asked.

Beckett shook his head. "Not right now. We'll talk about it later."

"Well, that's not ominous at all."

"What's ominous?" Brenna asked, pulling up to Beckett's side. She only had eyes for him, even though I was her best friend, but I let it be. It was fine that my best friend was in love with my brother. He had no idea, though maybe one day things would change, and something would happen. Still, Beckett was a little bit obtuse.

Beckett patted Brenna on the head, and I groaned.

Okay, he was a lot dense.

"You cut your hair. I like it."

"Did you just pat me on the head like a dog?" Brenna asked, huffing.

"What? It's cute."

She rolled her eyes, glared at me instead of him, and stomped away.

"What? What did I do?" Beckett looked honestly confused, and I wasn't going to enlighten him. It wasn't my place.

"I think you should probably go get a drink and just forget it."

"Fine," Beckett said and made his way towards where Brenna was, probably to either apologize or ask what he did wrong.

"Your family is loud," Eliza said, Lee at her side. My other best friend and Beckett's best friend had joined us as well and were mostly staying out of the way. I didn't blame them. We got loud when we were together, and it only got worse when Clay and the kids came. I loved the kids, though, and considering I knew for a fact that my father had egged them on for the game of tag, I didn't mind the noise.

"Hey, I'm glad you're okay," Lee said before kissing the top of my head.

I could feel a glare on me, and I knew Jacob was watching, but I ignored it. There was no reason for him to be jealous. Lee was a longtime friend, and I knew he'd never had eyes for me.

"Anyway, I need to head home soon," Eliza said quickly.

I looked up at her, frowning.

"Oh? We haven't even eaten."

"Marshall has a scheduled call soon, thankfully. I want to make sure I'm home for that."

Lee frowned. "Do you need a ride?"

She shook her head and smiled. "No, I'm fine. I drove here. And I made sure I was a little farther down the block so no one blocked me in. But I'm glad you're safe. Never do that again. You scared the life out of me." Eliza kissed me on the cheek, and I hugged her tight, and then Lee wrapped his arms around us both and lifted us up.

"What was that for?" I called out.

"I just felt like it," Lee said, gave us a wicked grin, and then went over to where the others were.

I shook my head, alone for a moment before Jacob came over and brushed my hair from my face before kissing me softly.

"I was about to beat up Beckett's little friend," he growled against my lips.

I wrapped my arms around his waist and sighed. "It's just Lee. You don't have to be jealous of him."

"I can be jealous of anybody I want," he said softly. "I love you," he whispered.

My heart squeezed, and I let out a happy sigh.

"I love you, too."

"There are a lot of people in this home that love you. A lot that are your family."

"Like your parents, and you." I paused. "Jonah's here, too, you know. Don't you feel it?"

I did my best to mention him often, to never forget, and I knew Jacob was doing the same. And when his eyes filled with the barest hint of sadness before he smiled, I knew I'd said the right thing.

"It's precisely what I was thinking. He's here, probably telling jokes, and wondering why it took us so long."

"I had to become me before I could find you."

"That's a very good answer," he whispered and kissed me again.

"Get a room!" Archer called.

"Or not," Dad corrected. "Let's sit down and act like civilized people and stop making out in corners. Both of my young ladies," Dad scolded, and Paige laughed until I pulled away, sliding my fingers along Jacob's.

"Well, you're about to be inundated by the full Montgomery experience. Are you ready for this?"

He winced. "I don't know if I'm ready for the Montgomerys, but I've always been ready for you. It just took me a little while to realize it."

I turned under my fiancé's arm and made my way to my family, connections and all. I knew that we might not be fully steady, we might have a little more broken bits than others, but we were finding our way.

One promise at a time.

BROKEN

Eliza

𝓘 set my phone and purse down on the table as I walked in and rolled my shoulders back. It was a fun party, seeing Annabelle so happy meant the world to me, but it was still hard to see others so ecstatic about their futures when mine wasn't home yet.

What an odd thing to say, considering it felt like I had spent more of my adult life alone than with my husband. But Marshall would be home soon. Within the next sixteen days.

I could not wait to see him.

It had been a long tour this time. Longer than all the others. And I hoped it would finally be the last. Between Marshall being on tour, and all four of my brothers being strewn across the world, I was tired of being alone. And though Annabelle and the others did their best to make sure

I was never truly alone, that I knew I had them as family, I wasn't entirely right yet.

I wasn't completely whole.

But soon, Marshall would be home, and then my brothers, and then everything would be okay. Finally.

I slid my earrings out of my ears, tossed my shoes onto the floor, and looked around my small home that didn't feel like mine yet. I was a military wife. I didn't get to put many things on the walls or put my finishing touches on everything until I knew that we would be in a place for a while. These past two tours had extended Marshall's duties here, which meant I had been in one place longer than planned. I'd been able to put down some roots with friends, and at least get a decent job. But I still hadn't made this place a home. I needed to change that, but not until Marshall was here. I didn't want to make too many changes unless he was back. That way, when he came home, it wasn't too much of a shock.

He would already have enough stress when he came back stateside. I didn't need to add to it by changing everything and decorating things he had no chance to voice his opinions on.

It would have been nice to have my big family close, to not feel as though it had been ages since I'd seen them. But soon, that would change. I was only a little jealous of Annabelle and her family, but then again, they'd opened their arms to me, and I was never alone when it came to them. They were always there, Annabelle and Paige and Brenna and the Montgomery brothers. They were loud, boisterous, and always had open arms, even if the older two brothers, the twins, glowered a lot most days.

I was thinking about taking a bath when the doorbell

rang. I frowned, wondering if maybe Annabelle had decided to check on me.

Or perhaps it was a salesperson who wanted to sell me exterminator services or water. They seemed to come around more often these days, and it annoyed me to no end. It would annoy Marshall even more, so maybe I should get one of those signs that most solicitors would ignore, but at least I could point at it and scowl instead of having to speak and open the door fully.

I looked through the side window and my knees went weak. But I didn't say anything. Maybe it wasn't what I thought it was.

Perhaps this was just a mistake.

I was Mrs. Marshall Strong, Eliza Wilder Strong. I could do this.

I opened the door to the uniformed officer, the man who must be a chaplain, and my knees gave out.

"Mrs. Strong?"

I could hear the words, and I knew what was coming, but everything just echoed as a keening wail sounded.

Mine.

And when the men spoke, I knew it was over.

Marshall was dead.

My husband was gone.

Next up in the Montgomery Ink series?
Beckett Montgomery finds his fate with Eliza in INKED
OBSESSION

WANT TO READ A SPECIAL **BONUS EPILOGUE** FEATURING
JACOB AND ANNABELLE **CLICK HERE!**

A NOTE FROM CARRIE ANN RYAN

Thank you so much for reading **INKED PERSUASION!**

This book was about second chances, making mistakes, and finding your path. I hope you loved their story as much as I do.

Next up in the Montgomery Ink series?

Beckett Montgomery finds his fate with Eliza in Inked Obsession. I know their book won't be easy, but it's what needs to be written.

And if you're new to my books, you can start anywhere within the my interconnected series and catch up! Each book is a stand alone, so jump around!

Don't miss out on the Montgomery Ink World!

- Montgomery Ink (The Denver Montgomerys)
- Montgomery Ink: Colorado Springs (The Colorado Springs Montgomery Cousins)
- Montgomery Ink: Boulder (The Boulder Montgomery Cousins)

- Gallagher Brothers (Jake's Brothers from Ink Enduring)
- Whiskey and Lies (Tabby's Brothers from Ink Exposed)
- Fractured Connections (Mace's sisters from Fallen Ink)
- Less Than (Dimitri's siblings from Restless Ink)
- Promise Me (Arden's siblings from Wrapped in Ink)
- On My Own (Dillon from the Fractured Connections series.)

If you want to make sure you know what's coming next from me, you can sign up for my newsletter at www. CarrieAnnRyan.com; follow me on twitter at @CarrieAnn-Ryan, or like my Facebook page. I also have a Facebook Fan Club where we have trivia, chats, and other goodies. You guys are the reason I get to do what I do and I thank you.

Make sure you're signed up for my MAILING LIST so you can know when the next releases are available as well as find giveaways and FREE READS.

Happy Reading!

The Montgomery Ink: Fort Collins Series:
Book 1: Inked Persuasion
Book 2: Inked Obsession
Book 3: Inked Devotion

Want to read a special **BONUS EPILOGUE** featuring Jacob and Annabelle **CLICK HERE!**

Want to keep up to date with the next Carrie Ann Ryan
Release? Receive Text Alerts easily!

Text CARRIE to 210-741-8720

ABOUT THE AUTHOR

Carrie Ann Ryan is the New York Times and USA Today bestselling author of contemporary, paranormal, and young adult romance. Her works include the Montgomery Ink, Redwood Pack, Fractured Connections, and Elements of Five series, which have sold over 3.0 million books worldwide. She started writing while in graduate school for her advanced degree in chemistry and hasn't stopped since. Carrie Ann has written over seventy-five novels and novellas with more in the works. When she's not losing herself in her emotional and action-packed worlds, she's reading as much as she can while wrangling her clowder of cats who have more followers than she does.

www.CarrieAnnRyan.com

ALSO FROM CARRIE ANN RYAN

The Montgomery Ink: Fort Collins Series:
Book 1: Inked Persuasion
Book 2: Inked Obsession
Book 3: Inked Devotion

The Promise Me Series:
Book 1: Forever Only Once
Book 2: From That Moment
Book 3: Far From Destined
Book 4: From Our First

The On My Own Series:
Book 1: My One Night
Book 2: My Rebound
Book 3: My Next Play

The Tattered Royals Series:
Book 1: Royal Line

The Ravenwood Coven Series:
Book 1: Dawn Unearthed

Montgomery Ink:
Book 0.5: Ink Inspired
Book 0.6: Ink Reunited
Book 1: Delicate Ink
Book 1.5: Forever Ink
Book 2: Tempting Boundaries
Book 3: Harder than Words
Book 4: Written in Ink
Book 4.5: Hidden Ink
Book 5: Ink Enduring
Book 6: Ink Exposed
Book 6.5: Adoring Ink
Book 6.6: Love, Honor, & Ink
Book 7: Inked Expressions
Book 7.3: Dropout
Book 7.5: Executive Ink
Book 8: Inked Memories
Book 8.5: Inked Nights
Book 8.7: Second Chance Ink

Montgomery Ink: Colorado Springs
Book 1: Fallen Ink
Book 2: Restless Ink
Book 2.5: Ashes to Ink
Book 3: Jagged Ink
Book 3.5: Ink by Numbers

The Montgomery Ink: Boulder Series:
Book 1: Wrapped in Ink

Book 2: Sated in Ink
Book 3: Embraced in Ink
Book 4: Seduced in Ink
Book 4.5: Captured in Ink

The Gallagher Brothers Series:
Book 1: Love Restored
Book 2: Passion Restored
Book 3: Hope Restored

The Whiskey and Lies Series:
Book 1: Whiskey Secrets
Book 2: Whiskey Reveals
Book 3: Whiskey Undone

The Fractured Connections Series:
Book 1: Breaking Without You
Book 2: Shouldn't Have You
Book 3: Falling With You
Book 4: Taken With You

The Less Than Series:
Book 1: Breathless With Her
Book 2: Reckless With You
Book 3: Shameless With Him

Redwood Pack Series:
Book 1: An Alpha's Path
Book 2: A Taste for a Mate
Book 3: Trinity Bound
Book 3.5: A Night Away
Book 4: Enforcer's Redemption

Book 4.5: Blurred Expectations
Book 4.7: Forgiveness
Book 5: Shattered Emotions
Book 6: Hidden Destiny
Book 6.5: A Beta's Haven
Book 7: Fighting Fate
Book 7.5: Loving the Omega
Book 7.7: The Hunted Heart
Book 8: Wicked Wolf

The Talon Pack:
Book 1: Tattered Loyalties
Book 2: An Alpha's Choice
Book 3: Mated in Mist
Book 4: Wolf Betrayed
Book 5: Fractured Silence
Book 6: Destiny Disgraced
Book 7: Eternal Mourning
Book 8: Strength Enduring
Book 9: Forever Broken

The Elements of Five Series:
Book 1: From Breath and Ruin
Book 2: From Flame and Ash
Book 3: From Spirit and Binding
Book 4: From Shadow and Silence

The Branded Pack Series:
(Written with Alexandra Ivy)
Book 1: Stolen and Forgiven
Book 2: Abandoned and Unseen
Book 3: Buried and Shadowed

Dante's Circle Series:

Book 1: Dust of My Wings

Book 2: Her Warriors' Three Wishes

Book 3: An Unlucky Moon

Book 3.5: His Choice

Book 4: Tangled Innocence

Book 5: Fierce Enchantment

Book 6: An Immortal's Song

Book 7: Prowled Darkness

Book 8: Dante's Circle Reborn

Holiday, Montana Series:

Book 1: Charmed Spirits

Book 2: Santa's Executive

Book 3: Finding Abigail

Book 4: Her Lucky Love

Book 5: Dreams of Ivory

The Happy Ever After Series:

Flame and Ink

Ink Ever After

Single Title:

Finally Found You